Clutching her daughter's picture, Lilly drifted off to sleep.

She dreamed of walking, her hand gently holding her daughter's. Of hope. Of a future Lilly hadn't even known that she wanted until she'd seen the photo of Megan. Her baby's smile. Her eyes.

Then the dream changed.

It became dark, and Lilly felt pressure on her face and chest. Painful, punishing compression that made her feel as if her ribs were ready to implode.

She fought the dream, shoved at the pressure with her hands and forced herself to wake up.

Her eyes flew open.

The darkness stayed. So did the suffocating sensation.

It was unbearable. She couldn't breathe. Couldn't speak. Couldn't move.

It took a moment to understand why. The darkness and the pressure weren't remnants of the dream. They were real. Because someone was shoving a pillow against her face. Suffocating her.

Someone wanted her dead.

DELORES FOSSEN

UNEXPECTED FATHER

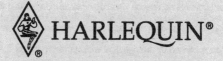

HARLEQUIN®

TORONTO • NEW YORK • LONDON
AMSTERDAM • PARIS • SYDNEY • HAMBURG
STOCKHOLM • ATHENS • TOKYO • MILAN • MADRID
PRAGUE • WARSAW • BUDAPEST • AUCKLAND

ISBN 0-373-88687-X

UNEXPECTED FATHER

This edition published by arrangement with Harlequin Books S.A.

® and TM are trademarks of the publisher. Trademarks indicated with
® are registered in the United States Patent and Trademark Office, the
Canadian Trade Marks Office and in other countries.

www.eHarlequin.com

Printed in U.S.A.

ABOUT THE AUTHOR

Imagine a family tree that includes Texas cowboys, Choctaw and Cherokee Indians, a Louisiana pirate and a Scottish rebel who battled side by side with William Wallace. With ancestors like that, it's easy to understand why Texas author and former air force captain Delores Fossen feels as if she was genetically predisposed to writing romances. Along the way to fulfilling her DNA destiny, Delores married a U.S. Air Force Top Gun who just happens to be of Viking descent. With all those romantic bases covered, she doesn't have to look too far for inspiration.

Books by Delores Fossen

HARLEQUIN INTRIGUE

Don't miss any of our special offers. Write to us at the following address for information on our newest releases.

Harlequin Reader Service
U.S.: 3010 Walden Ave., P.O. Box 1325, Buffalo, NY 14269
Canadian: P.O. Box 609, Fort Erie, Ont. L2A 5X3

CAST OF CHARACTERS

Lilly Nelson—She wakes up from a coma to learn she's given birth to a daughter, Megan, and that the unidentified person who tried to kill her still wants her dead. In order to protect her child, Lilly will have to depend on Megan's guardian...the very man she can't have, despite what her heart is telling her.

Detective Jason Lawrence—This tough-as-nails cop finds himself the unexpected father of his late brother's baby, Megan. Now, protecting Megan and Lilly from an unknown assailant could cost him everything, including his heart and his life.

Megan Nelson—She's still two weeks away from her first birthday and has no idea of the danger she's in. Megan only knows that she loves Jason and he's the only daddy she's ever known.

Wayne Sandling—A prominent, ruthless attorney who detests Lilly because of evidence she turned over to the police that got him disbarred.

Raymond Klein—Wayne Sandling's business associate whose career was also ruined with the evidence Lilly provided to the police. Is he willing to murder Lilly out of revenge?

Corinne Davies—Lilly's former secretary. On the surface Corinne seems helpful and supportive, but could she be covering her tracks to keep old secrets buried?

Erica Fontaine—She's been Megan's nanny since the day the child was born, and isn't happy to hand Megan over to Lilly.

Chapter One

St. Joseph's Convalescent Hospital
San Antonio, Texas

"Lilly came out of the coma." Dr. Staten's voice was clinical. Void of emotion or any speculation as to the impact of the bombshell that he'd just delivered.

Detective Jason Lawrence's reaction, however, wasn't quite so serene or detached.

There was emotion. Plenty of it. And speculation? That, too. A really bad kind of speculation that knotted his stomach and tightened every muscle in his body.

Oh, man.

It felt as if someone had sucker punched him.

"Lilly's awake?" Jason managed to ask even though he already knew the answer.

Still, he wanted a confirmation, and while he waited for it, he prayed.

Except he didn't know what the hell to pray for.

Dr. Staten nodded. "She woke up about two hours ago. That's why I called and asked you to come."

And at no time during the call had the doctor indicated that Lilly was no longer comatose. Of course, Dr. Staten probably thought it was news best delivered in person. Jason was debating that. Though there was nothing that could have helped pave the way for this, he would have liked a few minutes in private to prepare himself.

"How did this happen?" Because he didn't want to risk something as dignity-reducing as losing his balance, Jason dropped down into the burgundy leather chair across from Dr. Staten's desk.

"She simply woke up." The doctor lifted a shoulder and flexed his dark, gray-threaded eyebrows. "We don't know why. It's not a common occurrence, but it does happen—even after nineteen months."

Yes. These things probably did happen. But nineteen months had been more than enough time for Jason to believe it wouldn't happen.

Ever.

And he'd built his entire life around that *ever.*

Dr. Staten sat, as well, easing down into his chair, and from over the thin silver rims of his glasses, he examined Jason with sympathetic brown eyes. "I know this has to come as a surprise…"

Jason almost laughed. Not from humor. Definitely not from that. But from the irony. Lilly was awake—after nineteen months, three days and a couple of hours. After everyone, including the medical community, and he had given up hope. She was awake.

It was nothing short of a miracle.

And the beginning of what would no doubt be his own personal nightmare.

Jason pulled in his breath, released it slowly. "Has Lilly said anything?"

"A little. She's still somewhat disorientated and doesn't remember much about the car accident. That's to be expected. It'll take a while for her body to start functioning normally, but now that she's awake, I believe she'll make a full recovery."

Jason silently cursed his reaction. Cursed himself. And then cursed fate for dealing him a hand that he didn't want to play. He was happy for Lilly. Truly happy. No one deserved to be in a vegetative state, and now she would get a second chance at life. But Jason couldn't help it: her second chance changed everything.

"Have you told her?" Jason asked.

Dr. Staten paused a moment. There was no need for Jason to clarify his question; the doctor certainly knew what was foremost on his mind. "No. I figured it'd sound better coming from you."

Jason seriously doubted that. It wouldn't sound *better* coming from anyone. But it was true—he needed to be the one to tell Lilly.

So he could soften the blow.

So he could prepare her for the shock of her life.

And then what?

Would he ultimately lose everything that he'd come to love in the past year? Jason suddenly felt as if he were perched on top of a house of cards with an F-5 tornado bearing right down on him.

The doctor picked up a pen, groaned softly

and tossed it onto his desk. The cool facade was broken, and for the first time since Jason had walked into his office, he saw the frayed nerves.

Not exactly a comforting reaction.

"Lilly's expecting you," the doctor instructed. His suddenly strained voice said it all. "I let her know that you were coming."

And that was Jason's cue to get to his feet. He mustered what courage he could and tried to push aside his fears. No easy feat. His fears were mammoth, and the next few minutes would change his life forever.

"If you need more time, I can postpone the visit," Dr. Staten offered.

Man, was that tempting. But it wouldn't solve anything. This conversation with Lilly had to happen. Plus, delaying the inevitable would only prolong his agony.

Jason followed the doctor out of the office and toward the patient ward of the convalescent facility. With each step, his heart pounded and his breath thinned. Sheez. Such a wuss reaction. But he couldn't help it. Because he was a cop, his life had been on the line a couple of times, but he'd never before had this much at stake.

When they reached the room, the doctor stepped aside to allow Jason to enter ahead of him. Jason took a deep breath and pushed open the door to Lilly's room. A room he'd seen at least a dozen times. From the vantage point of the doorway anyway. He'd kept his distance, literally and figuratively. But this was different. She wasn't just lying there, eyes closed and attached to machines to monitor her vitals. One machine was still in place, as was an IV, but she was sitting up with the help of pillows stuffed behind her back.

Her gaze slid in his direction and she spotted him. Instant recognition. Jason knew that from the brief widening of her blue-green eyes followed by the not-so-brief tightening of her mouth.

"Jason," she said.

Not a friendly greeting. It dripped with questions. *Why are you here? Of all the people in the world, why would you be my first real visitor?*

Unfortunately, she would soon find out.

Because he suddenly felt awkward and fidgety, Jason stuffed his hands into the pockets of his khakis and ambled closer. "Welcome back, Lilly."

The right corner of her mouth lifted. "You actually seem sincere." Since her first attempt sounded as if she were speaking through gravel, she cleared her throat and repeated it.

"I am sincere."

And Jason was *almost* certain he believed that.

Lilly was pale, a skim-milk kind of pale, but other than that and the two-and-a-half-inch whitish scar angled on the left side of her forehead, she didn't look as if she'd been through a horrifying ordeal.

However, she did look different.

Her normally short auburn hair now lay on the tops of her shoulders. Loose. Not confined in one of the not-a-strand-out-of-place styles that she usually preferred. No makeup, either.

She had freckles and chapped lips.

Definitely not the pristine, polished corporate image that Jason had come to associate with that face. Too bad. Because that executive veneer had always been a reminder that she wasn't his type. That she was hands-off.

For reasons he didn't want to explore, she didn't seem so hands-off right now. Lilly seemed very small and vulnerable, despite her defensive expression and her smart-ass reply to his greeting.

"How are you?" he asked, mainly because he couldn't think of what else to say.

She hesitated as if considering what ulterior motive he might have for his question, and she moistened her lips. "Coming back from the dead isn't easy."

Jason nodded. "I imagine not."

Lilly made a you-don't-know-the-half-of-it sound. "My whole body's stiff, and it doesn't respond the way it should. I'll spare you most of the specifics, but I've got a wicked headache. Cotton mouth. And I understand it'll be days...or even longer before I can walk. I'm a little scared about that."

Lilly stopped, wrinkled up her forehead. And closed down. She was no doubt embarrassed that she'd revealed her fear of not being able to walk. It was a totally human, normal response, but Jason figured she would view it as a weakness.

"Of course, there's a bright side to this," she continued. It was her CEO presentation voice. Light, confident, airy. "I figure I've lost a lot of weight. I doubt I've been this thin since high school." Lilly fanned her trembling fingers through the air to indicate an imaginary marquee. "Coma—the ultimate diet."

"You'll be back to normal in no time," Jason promised her. Though he didn't know why. That certainly wasn't a promise he could deliver.

She stared at him a moment. "Oh, I get it now." Lilly's mouth relaxed and she made a clumsy swipe to push her rumpled hair off her forehead. "This is an official visit from *Detective* Jason Lawrence, San Antonio PD. You want to question me about the car accident that put me here in this hospital bed."

He wished that was the reason he'd come.

"I work Special Investigations now," Jason informed her. "Your accident doesn't come under the jurisdiction of my department."

Something, some raw emotion, rifled through her eyes. "So, you're here to talk about Greg." Lilly huffed and coupled it with a disapproving groan. "I figured you'd give me at least a day or two to catch up on current events, physical therapy, visits from friends, trips to Krispy Kreme, et cetera, before you started badgering me again about the night Greg died."

Greg. His brother. His *dead* brother. And the subject of the majority of Lilly's and his last conversations, and bitter arguments.

Always arguments.

It didn't matter that she was trying to diffuse this tension with her Krispy Kreme style of humor. The emotion and the pain were still there, crouching just below the surface of her words.

Jason moved closer and stopped a few inches from the foot of her bed. "I'm not here about Greg, either." Besides, no amount of questioning and arguments would bring his brother back. He knew that. *Now.* But Lilly was right—nineteen months ago, it'd been a topic he'd broached often with her.

And yes, there had been plenty of badgering involved.

"All right, then." She took a sip of water from a plastic cup clutched in her right hand. "You've piqued my interest. If you're not here to talk about Greg or my car accident, then this'll be a very short visit. Because I think we both know there's nothing else for us to discuss."

Jason couldn't fault her defensive attitude. He deserved it. After all, this was the woman he'd accused of contributing to the death of his brother. Despite the fact he'd known Lilly for more than six years before his brother's death, it was hard to stay friendly after an accusation like that. However, she was wrong about them having nothing else to discuss.

There was plenty.

"I'll give you two some privacy," Dr. Staten announced, and he stepped out of the room, shutting the door behind him.

Jason glanced over his shoulder to confirm the man's timely exit. Staten was definitely gone. The room suddenly seemed too small, and it was getting smaller by the second with Lilly's stare drilling into him. Where had the air gone?

"Do you remember anything that happened while you were in a coma?" Jason asked.

Lilly blinked, as if surprised by the question. "No." She paused. "In fact, not only is the coma a blank, so are the last few hours before I got into the car." She stopped, angled her head, studied him. "Is there something about the accident that the police are investigating?"

Jason chose his words very carefully.

"The case is still active. I'm sure the lead detective will want to question you when you're feeling up to it."

And he left it at that.

She made a soft *hmm* of agreement. And concern. "Then something must really be wrong for you to be here."

It was, and since there was no good introduction for what he had to tell her, Jason just started with the basics. "The night Greg was killed, you had sex with him."

Not a blink of surprise this time. More like a flash of anger over his bluntness. "I don't want to discuss this—"

"I know it happened because he called and told me. In fact, he told me just minutes before he died."

Since this was only a recap and since he hadn't wanted to start an argument with her, Jason left out one important detail: Greg had thought the sexual encounter might lead to a permanent relationship with Lilly rather than her shutting him out of her life.

But she had shut him out.

And because of that, Greg was dead.

There it was. The flood of old memories.

The still-fresh pain. Always the pain. Jason knew for a fact he wouldn't forget that grief any time soon. Nor would he forget, or forgive, what Lilly had done.

"Is this actually leading somewhere?" Lilly prompted in that crisp voice that he'd learned to hate. "Because I'm not in the mood for a trip down memory lane, especially when you're the one doing the navigating."

"It's leading somewhere." Since he needed it, Jason took another deep breath. "You got pregnant that night. With Greg's baby."

That got her attention. Man, did it ever. She did a double take and her breathing stilled. "Excuse me?"

"You got pregnant," Jason repeated. Because Lilly looked as if she badly needed it, and because he needed it, as well, he waited a couple of moments to give her some time to try to absorb that.

The plastic water cup started to collapse under the pressure of her grip. "I didn't know."

Jason had been afraid of that. So that meant Lilly was in for a double shock.

He'd have to save the third part of these

revelations for another day since that news would probably stall her recovery and send her into a panic.

A hoarse sob clawed its way past her throat. "Oh, God. Oh. God. Pregnant. I got pregnant." Her gaze slashed to his, and she groaned. "The accident caused me to miscarry, didn't it?"

Her reaction surprised him, and that was putting it mildly. Jason had been expecting her to be upset at the news of an unplanned pregnancy.

Or maybe that's how he'd hoped she would react.

Upset.

But this was a couple of steps past that particular emotion. He'd never thought of the workaholic, success-driven Lilly as overly eager to start a family, but she looked genuinely distressed over not just the pregnancy but the possibility of losing a child.

"No." Jason let her know. Not easily. But he finally got out the denial. "You didn't miscarry."

With her eyes suddenly dark and wide with concern, Lilly opened her mouth. Closed it. Frantically shook her head. "What do you mean *no*?" The question was all breath. Not a hint of sound. Yet Jason heard it clearly.

"Your injuries were mainly caused by a piece of metal railing that came through the windshield," Jason explained. "It hit you on the head, caused some major trauma. The airbag stopped any impact damage in your midsection and probably prevented you from miscarrying."

She didn't have much color in her face, but what was there, drained completely. Her bottom lip began to tremble. "I don't understand."

Jason waited a moment, until he stood a chance of his voice being steady. It wasn't a hundred percent, but under the circumstances, it was the best he could do. "You carried the baby full term, and then the doctors delivered it via C-section."

"Are you saying…" But she didn't finish. Mumbling something indistinguishable, she dropped back onto the pillows and her eyelids fluttered down.

Since Jason needed to end this conversation right here, right now, he just tossed it out there. Quickly. Before he could change his mind, turn and leave. "You had a baby, Lilly. Nearly a year ago."

She lay there. Not moving. Except for her lips. She continued to mumble something. A prayer, maybe. Then she opened her eyes. Slowly. As if she dreaded what she might see on his face.

"Had?" she repeated, obviously latching on to his use of the past tense. A tear streaked down her cheek.

A real honest-to-goodness tear.

In the six years he'd known her, he'd never seen Lilly cry. Oh, man. This was ripping them both to pieces—but for different reasons, of course.

Jason couldn't stand that look of undiluted pain on her face, so he put an end to it. "Not *had,* Lilly," he corrected. "You *have* a baby. A daughter."

Chapter Two

If it'd been any person other than Jason Lawrence telling her this, Lilly might have thought it was a joke. But this no-shades-of-gray cop wasn't the joking type. Heck, she wasn't even sure he was the smiling type. Still—

A baby.

How could that be?

If this was the truth, then she would have been…what? She quickly did the math. She would have been two months pregnant when she was involved in the car accident. Two months, as in sixty days.

Yet she hadn't known.

How could she have not known?

Her life had always been so organized. She'd known every appointment, every deadline. So, how could a missed period or two have escaped her notice?

Almost hysterically, Lilly slapped the plastic cup onto the table beside her bed so she could pinch herself. Hard. She felt it all right, the sting of the pressure on her skin. But that wasn't definitive. Maybe she was still in a coma. Maybe she was dreaming about a pinch and a pregnancy.

Yes.

That was it. This had to be some weird dream, even though she couldn't recall a single instance of a dream the entire time she'd been in a coma.

"It's for real," Jason volunteered as if he could hear the argument going on in her head.

He walked toward her, slowly, and held out his arm. Probably so she could touch him. Because she didn't know what else to do, Lilly took him up on that offer. She reached out. Dreading, hoping and praying all at the same time. Her fingertips brushed against the smooth fabric of his bronze-colored jacket, which was nearly the same color as his short, efficient hair.

The jacket felt like…well, a jacket.

But Lilly went one step further. She slid her fingers over the back of his hand. Warm, human skin. Comforting in a primal sort of way.

And maybe in other ways, too.

She suddenly wanted to latch on to his hand, and it wasn't totally related to her need to make sure she was truly conscious. Simply put, she needed a hug. Mercy, did she ever. Even though she was twenty-seven—no, make that twenty-nine—she suddenly felt as fragile as a newborn baby.

Ironic.

Since a baby was the exact topic of conversation that'd sent her heart and thoughts into a tailspin.

Lilly met Jason's gaze again, to see how he was reacting to all of this touching stuff, but whatever he was feeling, he kept it carefully hidden in the depths of those smoke-gray eyes. No surprise there. She'd always believed Jason was born to be a cop.

Or a professional poker player.

Because that rugged stoic face gave away nothing. The only time she'd ever seen an overt display of emotion from him was the night his brother, Greg, had died. Understandable. She'd had an overt display of her own.

Well, afterward, anyway.

When Jason had gone and she had been alone.

"Are you okay?" Jason asked.

Lilly didn't even consider a polite lie. "No. I'm not. It's hard to be okay when nothing makes sense."

She moved on to part three of the reality check. Not knowing what to hope she might see, Lilly clutched the hem of her roomy green hospital gown and jerked it up. Thank goodness she was wearing panties or Jason would have gotten a real eyeful. But even if she hadn't had on underwear, she would have looked anyway. She needed proof.

And she got it.

She slid her fingertips over the thin, pinkish-colored scar. Right on her lower abdomen. Not some ragged wound caused by an injury, but clearly the result of surgery.

A C-section.

Jason leaned in closer. So close. *Too* close. He caught her gown and eased it back into place so that the soft cotton whispered over her thighs. Probably because her near nudity bothered him.

No, wait.

He didn't think of her that way. He'd covered her probably because further examination wasn't necessary. She had all the proof she needed.

Reality check was over. Now it was time to deal with the aftermath. And she dealt, all right. The breath swooshed out of her and because she didn't want any tears to escape, Lilly squeezed her eyes shut.

"A daughter?" she said.

"Yes." Jason's voice was tight. Edgy. Exactly the way she felt.

He didn't add anything else, and it didn't take long for the smothering silence to settle uncomfortably between them. Lilly used that quiet time to try to put a stranglehold on her composure, to try to grasp what was happening.

But both were impossible tasks.

Only two hours earlier she'd awakened to learn that she'd lost nineteen months of life because of a car accident that she couldn't even remember. Nineteen months. Heaven knew what toll the coma had taken on her body. And there was the inevitable toll that her absence had no doubt taken on her business. Sweet heaven, she'd lost so much. Now, Jason had informed her that she'd been pregnant and delivered a baby.

A baby who was almost a year old.

"Her name is Megan," she heard Jason say.

At the sound of some movement, Lilly opened her eyes to find him searching through his wallet. He extracted something. A photograph that was a bit crumpled around the edges. He held it up so she could see it.

Her mouth went dry.

She took the picture, hesitantly, and pulled it closer to her so she could study it. The little girl had auburn hair. Not quite a genetic copy of Lilly's own, but close. Darn close. It wasn't straight but instead haloed her face in soft, loose curls. Just as Lilly's own hair had done when she was that age.

Lilly caught her bottom lip between her teeth to cut off any unwanted sound she might make. At this point, any sound would be unwanted. And too revealing.

In the photograph, Megan was smiling. Not a tentative one, either. It went all the way to her eyes.

"Oh, mercy," she whispered. Lilly pressed the picture to her chest.

This precious child was hers.

The connection she felt for Megan was instant. Not a gentle tug of her heart, either, but a feeling so intense, so right, that the tears she'd fought came anyway. Lilly didn't even care that she was losing control. Seeing that tiny face was worth all the tears. It was worth humiliating herself in front of Jason. Worth the coma.

Worth everything.

Her baby.

Her own flesh and blood.

"I've missed so much," she mumbled, knowing it was a total understatement. She'd missed carrying her child. Giving birth. And most importantly, she had missed nearly the entire first year of her daughter's life.

"Yes," Jason whispered.

Since there was a lot of emotion in his one-word comment, Lilly looked at him again. He still had on his cop's face, but those eyes said it all. Or at least they said *something*. Exactly what that *something* was, she didn't know.

Unless…

"She's Greg's baby," Lilly clarified. Why, she didn't know. She didn't need to explain her sex life to Jason.

He nodded. "The doctors did a DNA test on Megan after she was born."

What a waste of time. If Lilly had been awake during Megan's birth, she could have told them there was no reason for such a test. Before that night with Greg, it'd been nearly a year since she'd had sex. And that one time with Greg hadn't been unprotected, either, which meant something had gone wrong with the condom.

And then it hit her.

Her heart practically leaped to her throat. "Who has her? Both Greg's and my parents are dead—"

"I have her," Jason interrupted.

Lilly was surprised that her heart didn't jump right out of her chest. It was already pounding, and his statement made it pound even harder. "You?"

That improved his posture. Not that he needed it. He was already soldier-stiff, which was his usual demeanor, but Jason seemed to take her simple question as a challenge.

"Me," he enunciated through semi-clenched teeth.

Oh.

Even with his adamant confirmation, it just didn't register in her brain and was in total conflict with the image she had of Jason Lawrence.

He shoved his hands into his pockets; it seemed as if he changed his mind a dozen times as to what he was about to say. "You were in a coma so long that the doctors didn't think you would recover. *I* didn't think you'd recover. I was Megan's next of kin."

There was something in the way he said that. Especially the tone he used when he tossed out the last part. Next of kin. Something…territorial? Something that launched a flurry of mental speculation.

And it also launched an equal flurry of concern.

A moment later Lilly realized that her concern was warranted.

"I have custody of her," Jason finished. He paused a moment. "Legally, Megan is my daughter."

Chapter Three

Jason braced himself for Lilly's reaction. Or rather, he tried to. It was hard to brace himself for something he wasn't sure he could handle.

"Oh, God," Lilly mumbled. Not exactly the hostile accusation that he thought she might fire in his direction. After all, he'd just confessed to claiming her child. "You took Megan in. You've been raising her."

It was a lot more than that. Yes, he'd taken the child in. Yes, he was raising her. But he also loved her. More than life. More than anything.

And he couldn't lose her.

"I'll bet taking care of a baby required some serious lifestyle changes for you," Lilly commented. Not chitchat, though. Her eyes were too strained for that, and there was a slight tremble in her voice—which probably meant she was as thunderstruck as he was.

She'd just learned that she had a daughter.

And Jason had just learned that he might lose one.

"I made a few lifestyle changes," he admitted. He tried to rein in his feelings. Failed. "It was worth it. Megan's a sweet kid."

Now there was a reaction from Lilly. Something small and subtle. But he could almost see the realization come to her. She'd had a child, but for all practical purposes, she wasn't in the picture.

Jason didn't think it was much of a stretch that Lilly would soon want to change that.

"Well…" Lilly started. But she didn't finish whatever thought she'd intended to voice. Instead she looked down at the picture. She held it as if it were delicate crystal that might shatter in her hands. "She has my hair. Greg's eyes, though." She lifted a shoulder. An attempt at a nonchalant shrug. But there was nothing nonchalant about any of this. "Your eyes, too."

Yes. The infamous Lawrence gray eyes that seemed to be the equivalent of a mood ring. Silvery pearl, sometimes, and on those not-so-good *sometimes*—gunmetal and steel.

Megan had them in spades, along with the olive-tinged completion that was the genetic contribution from Greg's and his Hispanic grandmother. Megan was a Lawrence through and through.

But Jason could see Lilly in the child's face, too. The way Megan sometimes defiantly lifted her chin. The sly, clever smile that could melt away botched cases, heavy workloads, long hours at work and other unsavory things. At first, it'd been difficult for him to see the smile, Lilly's smile, on the mouth of the child he loved.

DNA sure had a bent sense of humor.

"I want to see her, of course," Lilly said.

It wasn't exactly a request, either. She certainly hadn't framed it with a please and hadn't left room for argument.

Though Jason wanted to argue.

Worse, he wanted to take Megan and run. To hide her so that he wouldn't lose her. But not only was that a stupid reaction, it would be wrong. He'd been the one to raise Megan—so far—but now that Lilly was awake and on the road to recovery, he no longer had sole claim to her.

Maybe he wouldn't have any claim at all.

And that sent a stab of pain straight through his heart.

"I'll make arrangements for you to see her," Jason offered, once he could speak. "When you're feeling up to it."

There was a flash of that sly smile, and it was tinged with sarcasm. "I think it's safe to say that I'll feel up to seeing her anytime, any place. After all, she is my daughter."

Jason had somehow known, and feared, that she would say that. "I just wasn't sure you'd want her to visit you here in the hospital."

It wasn't a lie. Exactly. That had crossed his mind. It'd also crossed his mind that he wanted to delay the visit so he could prepare Megan. How, he didn't know. It wasn't always easy to reason with a baby. But perhaps he could show Megan pictures of Lilly so she wouldn't be frightened of meeting a stranger who just happened to be her mother.

Picture recognition might help Megan. But it wouldn't do much to soothe his fears. Nothing could do that.

"Besides, it's late," Jason added. "Nearly six."

And he was babbling. Hell. He wasn't a babbler. Worse, he seemed to be grasping at straws, at anything, to postpone what he knew he couldn't postpone.

"All right," Lilly said. She kept her attention staked to him. "This definitely qualifies as an awkward moment. We're a lot closer to being enemies than we are friends, and yet you did this incredible, wonderful thing by taking in my—"

"Don't," Jason interrupted. He took a moment to gain control of his voice, and his temper, before he continued. "I don't want your thanks." He could handle her hostility, even her sarcasm, even that damn sly smile, before he could handle her gratitude. "I said I'd arrange for you to see Megan, and I will."

Lilly nodded. "I might not be reading you right, but I get the feeling there's something else. Something you're not telling me."

Well, the coma hadn't dulled her instincts. That was both good and bad news. He wanted Lilly to be healthy and on the road to recovery. He *truly* did. But Jason had been counting on having a few days or even weeks before having to tell her everything. Not just about Megan and his custody. Other things, like the events surrounding the night she'd nearly died.

Panic began to race through her eyes. "Is Megan okay? There's nothing wrong with—"

"Megan's perfectly healthy," he told her. "She's had normal childhood illnesses, of course. An ear infection. A cold or two. Nothing major."

The pulse on her neck was pounding so hard that Jason could actually see it. "However?" she questioned.

Yes, there was a *however.*

Jason considered the several ways he could go with this, including just ending the conversation and heading out. If he followed department regulations to a tee, he should just turn this over to the lead detective. But he couldn't do that to Lilly. Despite their past and the inevitable obstacles they would no doubt face in the future, there was some information she needed to know.

The operative word was *some.*

Jason groaned and scrubbed his hand over his face. "The police will want to question you about the car accident."

Her brief silence probably meant she was processing that. Not just his comment but his groan, as well. She leaned closer. So close that he could see all those swirls of blue and green in her eyes. "Are you saying they weren't able to figure out what happened?"

It was touchy territory and, as Jason had done several times during their conversation, he considered his answer carefully. "They'll want an eyewitness statement to the incident, and you're the ultimate eyewitness. It's standard procedure." He hesitated, gathered his breath. "They also want to talk to you about the information you found when you were going through your father's old business records."

"You mean, the computer files that implicated some people in my father's dirty dealings?" Lilly didn't wait for him to confirm that. "I remember copying those files to a CD."

"Yes. You'd called a friend in S.A.P.D. and told him about them."

"Sergeant Garrett O'Malley." Lilly touched her fingers to her left temple and massaged it gently. At first. Then, as the frustration began to show on her face, her massage got a little harder until her fingers pressed into her skin.

"After I copied the files, things get a little fuzzy."

Jason latched right on to that because even though her memory might not be totally intact, she still might be able to provide them with some critical details. "Just how fuzzy is fuzzy?"

"A big, giant blur." The temple massage obviously wasn't working so she stopped and huffed. "Did I give the CD to Sgt. O'Malley?"

He shook his head. "But you'd planned to do that the next morning."

She bobbed her head in an almost frantic nod. "Now I remember. I took the CD from my computer at the office and got into my car in the parking lot." Lilly froze. Her gaze froze, too, for several long moments before slowly coming back to his. "The CD wasn't with me when I had the accident?"

"No." This conversation was quickly taking them into uncomfortable territory. Because of their history together and because it didn't fall under his department, the best thing he could do was to back away. He definitely shouldn't be the one to interrogate her. "Look, you have enough to deal with right now—"

"And stalling won't help me deal with it any faster, okay? Tell me what's wrong, Jason."

He couldn't. The timing sucked, and whether Lilly believed it or not, she wasn't strong enough, mentally or physically, to hear the truth.

"You're still stalling," Lilly pointed out.

Yes, he was.

And he would continue to do so until he'd taken care of a few things. Such as security, for instance. At a minimum, he wanted a guard posted outside her room. Just as a precaution, especially since no one other than the medical staff and he knew that she was out of the coma. Then he needed to get the doctor's approval to allow the lead detective to tell Lilly what would essentially be yet another bombshell. One even bigger than the one he'd already delivered.

Because nineteen months ago, Lilly's car accident hadn't really been an accident.

In fact, Jason was about a hundred percent certain that someone had tried to murder her.

THE ROOM was too quiet.

No voices. No doctors. And definitely no

Jason. He'd left hours ago with a promise to return. Lilly repeated his words now, using the Terminator's thickly accented voice, and she added a hollow laugh.

God, how Jason must hate her.

First, there was her part in Greg's death. Or from Jason's perspective, not her part. She was *entirely* responsible. She accepted that. She *was* responsible. And no amount of penance, wishing or grieving would bring Greg back.

Nothing would.

Of course, Jason now had a new reason to despise her: Megan. He no doubt saw her as a threat to his custody. That was true, as well, a realization that didn't make Lilly feel like issuing even a hollow laugh. This would almost certainly turn into a long battle where there would be no winners, least of all her daughter.

Lilly tried to force her eyes to stay open. Hard to do, though. If the clock was accurate on her bed stand, it was already past midnight, the end of what had been one of the most exhausting days of her life.

She could blame the fatigue in part on the physical therapy that she'd demanded. A two-hour session. Grueling. Painful. Essentially she'd discovered during the session that her muscles felt like pudding and were just about as useful. It would take "lots of time and hard work," the physical therapist had said, for her to regain complete use of her limbs.

Lilly didn't mind the hard work, but she wouldn't settle for the *lots of time.*

She planned to be walking by the end of the week.

It wasn't exactly an option, either. She needed to be mobile so she could see her daughter. She wanted to start building a life with the child she hadn't even known existed until six hours ago.

A child she already desperately loved.

She hugged the picture to her chest and tried to stave off the tears. She failed. They came anyway. Tears of joy and sadness. The joy was there because she had a precious little daughter. The sadness, because she'd already missed so much of her baby's life.

She wouldn't miss anything else.

Thanks to Jason, her baby had apparently been well cared for—by the last man on earth whom she thought would do her any favors. Of course, Megan was his flesh and blood, as well. Greg's daughter. Jason's niece. That was probably the real reason he'd stepped up to the fatherly plate. He'd loved his brother. Therefore, he'd love his brother's child.

In spite of the fact that Megan was her child, too.

There was true irony in that. Her sworn enemy had her daughter. Not just *had* her, either. Jason was her legal custodian. A father by law. And he was the only parent Megan had ever known. It wouldn't be easy for her to try to find her place in her baby's life.

But she did have a place.

And no matter how hard it was, she would find it.

Her eyelids drifted down again, but she fought it. It was irrational, but the thought of sleep actually terrified her. Because she might not wake up. Because she might lapse into another coma and stay there. In a permanent vegetative state. Alive in name only.

"That won't happen," Dr. Staten had promised her when he'd checked on her after the physical therapy session.

However, Lilly hated to take the chance.

Still, she couldn't stop her eyes from shutting. She couldn't stop the fatigue from taking over. And the quietness of the room and the night closed in around her.

Clutching her daughter's picture, she drifted off to the one place she didn't want to go: sleep.

She dreamed of walking, her hand gently holding her daughter's. Of hope. Of a future Lilly hadn't even known she'd wanted until she'd seen the photo of Megan. Her baby's smile. Her eyes.

Then the dream changed.

It became dark and Lilly felt pressure on her face and chest. Painful, punishing pressure that made her feel as if her ribs were ready to implode.

She fought the dream, shaking her head from side to side. When that didn't work, she shoved at the pressure with her hands and forced herself to wake up.

Her eyes flew open.

The darkness stayed.

So did the god-awful pressure.

It was unbearable. She couldn't breath. Couldn't speak. Couldn't move.

It took a moment to understand why. The

darkness and the pressure weren't remnants of the dream. They were real. Very real. Because someone was shoving a pillow against her face. Suffocating her.

Someone wanted her dead.

Chapter Four

The panic and the adrenaline knifed through Lilly, hot and raw. It was instant. Like a fierce jolt that consumed her. Fight or flight.

Do whatever it takes to survive.

Lilly managed to make a muffled, guttural sound. It wasn't quite a scream, but she prayed it was loud enough to alert someone. Anyone. And she began to flail her arms at her attacker. She fought. Mercy, did she ever fight. She wouldn't just let this SOB kill her. But her pudding-like muscles landed as helpless thuds on the much stronger hands that were smothering her.

Who was trying to kill her?

Better yet, how could she stop it from happening?

Even over the pounding of her heartbeat and the rough sounds of the struggle, she heard the footsteps. Frantic. Fast. Someone was coming.

Just like that, the pressure stopped. Lilly didn't waste any time. She immediately shoved the pillow aside and, starved for air, gulped in several hard breaths so she wouldn't lose consciousness.

She quickly looked around to make sure her attacker wasn't still here. The room was pitch-black. Well, maybe. She couldn't tell if the darkness was real or some leftover effect from nearly suffocating.

"I need help," she called out.

The footsteps merged and blended with others, until Lilly was no longer able to distinguish which were coming and which were going.

"Hell," someone said.

Jason.

He ran to her bed and looked down at her. He made a split-second check, probably to make sure she was still alive and well. The *alive* part was true, but it might be eternity before she could achieve the *well* part. She was shaking from head to toe and was on the verge of losing it.

Jason already had his standard-issue

police Glock drawn, and he whipped his aim around the room. Ready to fire at the intruder.

But no one was there.

On the far end of the room, the window was open and the gauzy white curtains fluttered in the night breeze. It would have been a tranquil scene if a would-be killer hadn't just used it as an escape route.

Jason raced to the window, and while still maintaining his vigilant cop's stance, he checked outside. Cursed again. He used his cell phone to request assistance. His hard voice echoed through the room and her head.

"Are you okay?" he asked, hurrying back to her.

Lilly tried to take a quick inventory of her body. "I think so." But she had no idea if that was true.

"We can't stay here," Jason informed her.

He reached down and scooped her into his arms. Not a loving act. Far from it. Clutching her against his chest, he rushed her out of the room. Probably in case her attacker returned.

A truly horrifying thought.

She didn't want the person to get away, but

Lilly wasn't ready for round two, either. She was, however, ready for an explanation, and she was fairly sure that Jason was the person to give it to her.

"Earlier you were stalling about telling me something," Lilly said. Her teeth began to chatter and she suspected she might be going into shock. Great. As if she didn't have enough to deal with. Well, the shock would have to wait. She needed answers. "And I think that 'something' is important, that it has to do with what just happened."

"Yeah." Jason took her up the hall and to the deserted nurses' station.

"Yeah?" she repeated, amazed and frustrated that he'd dodged her question once again. "The time for stalling is over, don't you think?"

Jason deposited her onto a burgundy leather sofa in the small lounge just behind the nurses' station. The cool, slick leather didn't help with the chills that had already started.

With his own breath coming out in rough, frantic gusts, he glanced down at her. Just a glance. Before he turned his attention back to the doorway. Standing guard. Protecting her. Or rather, trying to.

"W-well?" Lilly prompted, curling up into as much of a fetal position as her stiff muscles would allow. "Don't you have something to tell me? Wait—let me rephrase that. You *have* something to tell me, so do it."

He nodded, eventually. "Your car accident probably wasn't an accident."

She watched the words form on his lips. Tried to absorb them. Couldn't. It was next to impossible to absorb that someone wanted her dead, especially since she couldn't recall anything about what had happened to her nineteen months ago.

"And what about tonight?" Lilly asked, afraid to hear the answer. "What happened?"

"This obviously wasn't an accident, either." Jason's jaw muscles stirred as if they'd declared war on each other. "Whoever tried to kill you nineteen months ago—I think he's back."

WHEN HE SAW the lanky, blond-haired detective making his way up the hall toward him, Jason ended the call with his lieutenant and stepped out of the doorway to Lilly's new room. He wanted to give his fellow S.A.P.D. peace officer his undivided attention. Unfortunately, it would be next to impossible to do that because of what the lieutenant had just requested.

Or rather, what the lieutenant had *ordered* him to do.

Talk about the ultimate distraction. That order kept repeating itself through Jason's head, and he doubted it'd go away any time soon. Especially since he had no clue as to how he could carry it out.

"Please tell me you have answers," he said to Detective Mack O'Reilly. Jason kept his voice low so he wouldn't wake Lilly. To get her to fall asleep, it'd taken nearly a half hour of questions and assurances from him that she was safe. Jason didn't want to go through that again until he could make good on those assurances.

If that were even possible.

O'Reilly shrugged. "I have answers, but I don't think you'll like them. There's only one surveillance camera in or around this entire place. It's in the parking lot and static, fixed in only one direction."

Jason tried not to curse. "Let me guess— the wrong direction?"

"You got it. It was aimed at the center of

the parking lot. Someone came up from the side and, while staying out of the line of sight, smashed the lens with a rock. All we got for a visual was a shadow. The crime-scene guys are dusting both the camera and the rock for prints, but it looks clean. Whoever it was probably had on gloves."

Definitely not good. Jason had hoped for a sloppy crime scene, even though deep down he'd known it wouldn't be. Whoever was behind this was brazen. Yes. Determined— that, too. Maybe even downright desperate.

But not sloppy.

Jason had personally gone over every inch of Lilly's room and hadn't found even trace evidence.

"How about the rookie guarding Ms. Nelson's room?" Jason asked. "Did you find him?"

O'Reilly nodded. "He was in the utility closet at the end of the hall. Duct tape on his mouth, hands and feet. He has a goose-egg-size lump on his head, and someone had used a stun gun on him, but he can't remember being knocked out."

Probably because the guard had fallen asleep.

This time, Jason didn't even try to contain his profanity, but it was aimed just as much at himself as it was at the guard. When Jason had checked on him about a half hour prior to Lilly's attack, the guy had looked a little drowsy. Jason had asked if he'd wanted to be relieved, but he'd said no, that the double espresso he was sipping would keep him awake all night.

Yeah, right.

Jason wanted to kick himself. Hard. How could he have let this happen?

He'd been positive that nineteen months ago someone had tried to kill Lilly. That's why he'd had a guard assigned to the convalescent hospital in the first place. What he should have anticipated, however, was that one guard wouldn't be enough. After all, the person responsible for this latest attempt on Lilly's life had no doubt been the one who'd forced her off the road and left her for dead.

Getting past one guard in the middle of the night obviously hadn't been much of a challenge. Murdering Lilly wouldn't have been a challenge, either, if Jason hadn't returned to the hospital to talk to Lilly's doctor about additional security measures for the facility.

Ironic.

While he'd been discussing the need for extra security, someone had been breaching it. And Lilly had nearly paid for that breach with her life.

"So far, no witnesses," O'Reilly continued. "But we're canvassing the neighborhood. Something might turn up."

Not likely. It was late. Midweek. The small downtown hospital was surrounded by specialty shops that mainly did business from ten to six o'clock. That meant there probably weren't a lot of potential witnesses milling around to see someone escaping through a window.

"I gave one of the detectives the names of two suspects, Wayne Sandling and Raymond Klein," Jason explained. "Both are former attorneys. About two years ago, Lilly uncovered some information that caused them to be disbarred."

What she'd uncovered, though, wasn't an offense that would have earned them jail time. While Sandling and Klein had been working as advisors to the city council, the two had somehow managed to get a construction company a lucrative contract to renovate historic city-owned buildings. The problem? The owners of the construction company were Sandling and Klein's friends. A definite conflict of interest. That suspicious contract wasn't enough for an arrest and, coupled with other similar unethical activity, it was barely enough to get them disbarred and fired as city council advisors.

But Jason knew there was more.

His brother, Greg, had even suspected it. After dealing with Sandling and Klein on a city contract deal, Greg too had noticed inconsistencies with bid dates and altered estimates that had ultimately cost him a contract to do auditing work for the city. Greg had been more than ready to request an investigation into the two attorneys' dealings. It hadn't happened, of course.

Because Greg had died in the car accident.

"Sandling and Klein have already been contacted," O'Reilly assured him. "Neither seemed pleased about that."

"I'll bet not. I want them questioned— hard."

"Absolutely."

Not that it would do much good. Questioning them hadn't been effective nineteen months ago. Jason had no doubts about Sandling's and Klein's guilt as far as unscrupulous business practices, but what was missing was solid proof that their unscrupulousness had gone much deeper than what the police had already found. There was no remaining evidence since the files that Lilly had copied from her computer had disappeared the night she'd been run off the road.

Jason knew that wasn't a coincidence.

Detective O'Reilly craned his neck to peer over Jason's shoulder. "By the way, how's Ms. Nelson?"

"Other than a few bruises, she wasn't hurt physically."

He couldn't say the same for her mental health, though. Here she was, only hours out of a coma. Hours where she'd learned she had a daughter that she hadn't even known she'd conceived. That in itself was enough trauma to face, but Lilly now had to deal with the aftermath of an attempted murder and a full-scale police investigation.

Jason looked back at Lilly, as well, and saw that she was in the exact place he'd left her. Well, sort of. She was still in the hospital bed. Still asleep. But it wasn't a peaceful sleep by any means. Her arm muscles jerked and trembled as if she were still in a fight for her life.

Which wasn't too far from the truth.

Someone wanted her dead, and wanted it badly enough to have tried not once but twice. Jason had been a cop for nearly eleven years and had learned a lot about criminal behavior.

This guy wasn't going to give up.

But then, neither was Jason.

It'd been a mistake not to beef up security, a bigger mistake to let down his guard, and he wouldn't do that again.

"Who knew Ms. Nelson was out of the coma?" O'Reilly asked.

It was a question Jason had already asked the hospital staff, and he'd gotten answers that hadn't pleased him. "Too many people. One of the nurses called a few friends to tell them the news. Another nurse called Lilly's former secretary—again, to share the good news. The doctors spoke to colleagues. Even Lilly's insurance company was contacted."

Jason couldn't consider himself blameless, either. He'd told Megan's nanny, Erica, though he didn't think Erica would pass on the information to anyone. And of course, there'd been paperwork processed at headquarters to assign the cop to security detail outside Lilly's room. In others words, at least several dozen people had learned that Lilly was no longer in a coma, and obviously one of those *several dozen* was someone who wanted her dead.

Lilly stirred again, and this time her eyes opened. In the same motion, she sat up, spearing him with her gaze. Her eyes were wild. Her breath, racing. She scrambled back toward the wall, banging into it with a loud thud.

O'Reilly immediately stepped away. "I'll let you know what the crime-scene guys say about the security camera." With that, the detective made a hasty exit, leaving Jason to deal with Lilly.

There was just one problem. Jason didn't know how to deal with her.

Seemingly disgusted with herself, she shook her head. "I keep dreaming."

Nightmares, no doubt. Jason wanted to tell her that they would go away, but he'd fed her enough lies tonight. Reassurances that she was safe didn't contain even a shred of truth.

Not yet, anyway.

Jason eased the door shut and walked to her. He had a ten-second debate with himself before he moved even closer and sat beside her on the bed. Yes, there was plenty of bad blood between them, but he would have had to be a coldhearted jackass not to try to offer some comfort.

"You have more bad news?" she asked, her voice cracking on the last word.

She was trembling all over, and he reached out. He pushed aside any doubts he had about what he was doing and pulled her into his arms. Lilly stiffened at first. Not a little stiffening, either, but a posture change that affected practically every muscle in her body. Probably because she was shocked by his gesture. Or maybe even appalled. But by degrees, she soon settled against him, as if she belonged there.

Jason quickly dismissed that last thought. Lilly didn't belong in his arms. She didn't belong this close to him. This was an anomaly. An emotional blip created by the dangerous situation that had forced this temporary camaraderie between them.

Then he felt her warm breath brush against

his neck. He took in her scent. The logic of emotional blips and anomalies flew right out the window.

Hell.

What was going on here?

The confusing yet tender episode lasted only a few seconds—thank God—because Lilly pulled back slightly and looked up at him. She squinted her eyes and appeared to be as thunderstruck as he felt.

Jason totally understood her dumbfounded state. Twenty-four hours earlier if someone had told him he'd be holding Lilly, and reacting to it in the most basic way a man could, he would have never believed it.

She swallowed hard and inched back even farther. The confusion in her eyes faded, and in its place came the uncomfortable realization of what had just happened.

Oh, yeah. They were on the same page.

Lilly cleared her throat, reached for the blanket and gave it an adjustment that it in no way needed. "You never did say—why were you here at the hospital tonight?"

Blind luck. But Jason kept that to himself. "I couldn't sleep, so I decided to drop by to check on the guard," he said, thankful for the conversation. It would hopefully take his mind off that *basic male* reaction he was still having. "When I saw Dr. Staten was still here, I went into his office to talk to him."

She paused. "Well…thank you."

Her thanks was genuine. Jason didn't doubt that. But he also didn't doubt that it hadn't been an easy thing for her to say to him. Civility of any kind was tricky between two battle-scarred enemies.

"I'm sorry," Lilly whispered, pulling away completely from him.

Jason immediately felt the loss of her body heat. A sensation that surprised and sickened him. Sheez. What the heck was wrong with him, anyway?

"What are you sorry for?" he managed to ask just to keep the discussion going.

"For borrowing your shoulder to cry on." She dusted her fingers across his jacket as if to remove any evidence of herself.

"After the scare you had, you deserve a shoulder, and the crying."

She stared at him. Paused. Stared at him some more. "You're being nice to me."

True, and he wasn't exactly pleased that she'd pointed it out. "Blame it on the adrenaline and fatigue." He groaned softly. "Don't worry… I'll be back to normal in no time."

"Good," she concluded. "Because it's easier that way."

Jason nodded, understanding. They had enough to deal with without bringing Greg's death and all those unresolved issues to the table. Unfortunately, one of those issues now seemed to be this bizarre attraction, or whatever the heck it was, that he felt for her.

Lilly leaned back, rested her head against the stack of pillows. "I wish I'd at least gotten a glimpse of the person who tried to smother me. Maybe I would have recognized him so you could arrest him."

Jason almost blew out a breath of relief at the change of subject. The *right* change. Too bad he hadn't thought of it sooner. Which only showed how dangerous distractions could be. Instead of pondering the effect of his hormones, he should be questioning her and digging for any clues to help them find the perp.

"A visual isn't the only way to recognize someone," he reminded her. "Was there anything familiar about his scent or his clothes?"

She immediately shook her head. "No."

Jason continued to press. "How about his voice? Did he say anything?"

"No to all of those. No scent. I wasn't able to touch his clothes. And if he said anything, I didn't hear it." Lilly paused a moment. "I can't even be sure it was a man. All I know is the person was a lot stronger than I am." She flexed her eyebrows. "But then, I'm not exactly a menacing threat with my super-heroine strength, am I now? It didn't take much to subdue me."

So they weren't necessarily looking for a male, strong or otherwise. Just someone who had a reason to kill her. And Jason knew for a fact there were people who fit right into that category. "This has to be connected to your father. To his dirty business dealings."

"I agree. He was involved in so much. Falsifying paperwork and bids so he'd get contracts for services that he then only partially provided…if at all. He scammed a lot of people with bogus agreements to do everything from audits to major construction." Lilly grabbed a handful of the blanket and fisted it until her knuckles whitened. "He's been dead for two and a half years. You'd think the fallout would be finished by now."

It wouldn't be finished until this SOB was caught. "We still have the same suspects. Names we've gone over hundreds of times."

"And it could also be any one of the dozens of former business associates that my father scammed or involved in his illegal schemes. Once I'm back on my feet, I want to go through my office and my house—" Her eyes widened. "I still have an office and house, don't I?"

He nodded. "Your attorney's been taking care of that with money from your personal and business accounts. But it probably won't do any good to visit your house and office. The police went through them and didn't find anything."

"Maybe they missed something." She froze, and her gaze whipped back to his. "Oh, my God. Megan. What if this person tries to go—"

"There's a cop at my house." One he could trust not to fall asleep. He wasn't about to risk Megan's life.

Lilly's breath was racing now and she placed her hand on her chest. "Thank you, again."

Jason decided it was a good time to get to his feet and put some distance between them. Unlike Lilly's other thanks, this one didn't feel so warm and fuzzy. Nothing he did for Megan required gratitude. What he did for her was totally out of love, and it riled him that Lilly even felt that she had a right to thank him.

Yes, it was stupid. Petty, even. But every paternal instinct in his body screamed for him to latch on to Megan and not let Lilly anywhere near her. He would have to override his instincts, though.

His lieutenant hadn't given him much of a choice about that.

"I'm making arrangements for you to be transferred to another hospital," Jason advised her. "Logistically, this one just isn't that easy to secure."

"And then what?" she asked, her voice thin. "I'd planned to be discharged in a day or two."

He'd already considered that, along with the lieutenant's order. "Once the doctors release you, you'll be placed in protective custody. *My* protective custody."

"Oh." Something flickered in her eyes and she stayed quiet a moment. "Let me guess— that wasn't your idea?"

"My lieutenant's," he admitted.

Another *Oh.* "How in the world did he convince you to agree to that?"

"Quite easily. He reminded me that Megan might need protection, as well, and that I'd no doubt want to be the one to provide it."

She examined him with her firm gaze. "This way, you kill two birds with one stone."

The word "kill" turned his stomach. "I don't like that analogy." But to protect both Lilly and Megan and to minimize the disruptions to Megan's life, the thing to do was for Lilly to move in with him.

It was logical.

Mercy, he hated that frickin' word.

The move was *logical,* but nothing else about this was. This was the next step in the nightmare he'd dreaded since the moment he'd heard that Lilly had come out of the coma.

He would literally put Lilly under the same roof with the daughter he loved more than life itself.

The daughter she'd no doubt try to take from him.

Lilly shook her head. "You know this protective custody won't work, right?"

Jason shrugged. "We don't have a choice."

"Maybe we do. I could always use a private bodyguard."

Jason was about to give her an opinion on that, and it wasn't a good opinion, but something—or rather someone—stopped him.

"I will see her now!" someone yelled from the hall. It was a man's voice. One that Jason didn't immediately recognize. That angry shout had him moving and reaching for his weapon.

"Take another step," he heard Detective O'Reilly warn, "and I promise you'll regret it."

With his gun ready and aimed, Jason hurried to the door and looked out. Hell. While he hadn't recognized the voice, he certainly recognized the man.

Wayne Sandling.

The former prominent attorney who'd done business with Lilly's father. Lots of business. And it hadn't all been aboveboard, either. Sandling was the last person on earth Jason wanted near Lilly.

"He barged his way in through the front desk," O'Reilly told Jason.

That didn't please Jason, but he would

deal with the lax security once he'd finished with Sandling. "What are you doing here?" Jason demanded.

Sandling obviously recognized him, as well, because the man's mouth practically curled into a snarl. "Detective Lawrence. Long time, no see."

It wasn't nearly long enough.

Though the former attorney had no doubt climbed out of bed to make this visit, he somehow managed to look as if he were ready for the courtroom. He wore a navy suit, complete with a tie. A tie! At this hour of the morning. His ink-black, conservative-cut hair had been combed to perfection. Not even a hint of sleep was in his eyes. For someone that meticulous, it made Jason wonder how he'd managed to get caught doing anything illegal in the first place.

"You didn't answer my question, Sandling," Jason pointed out. "Why are you here?"

"Isn't it obvious?"

"Not really." Jason used his best badass-cop voice and added a glare. "Clarify it for me."

If Sandling had an unsavory response to

Jason's tone and glare, he didn't show it. "One of your fellow officers called me tonight. About an attack on Lilly Nelson. He wanted to know if I had an alibi."

"Do you?"

"That's not the point. The point is I was awakened and questioned." His cosmetically perfect teeth came together for a moment. "I don't like that."

"Well, I don't like someone trying to kill Ms. Nelson." Jason stepped closer, making sure he violated Sandling's personal space. "So, where were you tonight?"

"Home, in bed, asleep. Alone," he added. Sandling came closer, too, violating Jason's personal space. "And I won't be questioned about my every move, either."

"You don't have a choice about that. You have motive and that gives me the right to question you about your *every move*."

"Is that Wayne Sandling?" Lilly called.

"Don't you dare try to get out of bed," Jason warned her without taking his eyes off the man. He didn't want Lilly to have to confront Sandling. That didn't mean she'd agree with him, and she would probably go so far as to try to get up and make her way into the hall.

That wasn't going to happen.

Jason decided it was time to put an end to this spur-of-the-moment conversation. "Detective O'Reilly, escort Mr. Sandling out of the building. If he puts up a fight, arrest him."

"I won't let the cops and Lilly Nelson try to pin trumped-up charges on me again," Sandling insisted. "Find another scapegoat, Detective Lawrence, and leave me the hell alone."

And with that, Sandling turned and walked away. His hand shot up, to give O'Reilly a back-off warning when the detective tried to take hold of his arm. O'Reilly's escort duty wasn't necessary; Sandling left on his own, practically gliding down the hall. Jason kept his gaze fastened on him until the man was out of sight.

"Make sure he doesn't come back," Jason instructed O'Reilly. He turned to Lilly, who was indeed trying to get out of bed. "Stay put. He's gone."

Huffing, Lilly sank her head back onto the pillow. "Well, that was a special ending to a special night."

It was indeed. "I'll beef up security at the nurses' station and the front door." Just having to say that riled him, because until

Sandling's impromptu visit, Jason thought he'd already done that. Which only proved just how dangerous this situation was. It was next to impossible to secure the place. He needed to have her transferred to the other hospital immediately.

"Sandling wouldn't dare try to come back tonight," Lilly said under her breath.

It seemed as if she was trying to convince herself.

"Are you still having doubts as to whether you need protective custody?" Jason didn't wait for her answer. "Then think again. Because I'm going to protect you whether you want it or not."

It was an order. Solid. Forceful. Certain. But Jason had his own doubts about the certainty. With everything that'd happened, he had to wonder. Could he do his job and keep Lilly alive?

Chapter Five

Lilly's nerves were too frayed, and there were too many butterflies in her stomach for her to object to what Jason was doing. And what he was doing was lifting her from her wheelchair into the seat of the waiting SUV he'd rented. The rental was a necessity, he'd insisted, because his own vehicle would be too easily recognized.

By Wayne Sandling, perhaps.

Or by someone else who wanted to silence her permanently.

Carrying her was a necessary act, as well, Lilly reminded herself, because despite the past two days of intensive physical therapy, she still wasn't able to walk unassisted. That meant she didn't have a choice about his *hands-on* care. Still, there was something unnerving about having to rely on anyone—

especially Jason—to make sure she got from point A to point B.

On the plus side, she was leaving point A: the hospital.

Point B: Jason's house.

Where she would see her daughter for the first time.

Lilly glanced down at the photo she had cradled in her hand. That instantly soothed the unpleasantness from having to rely on Jason to carry her. It also lessened the fatigue and the stress from the spent adrenaline and the sleepless nights. She could face almost anything now that she knew she'd soon meet Megan.

The April air was already muggy and much too warm, and the morning breeze whipped at them, bringing with it the fruity grape smell of some nearby mountain laurels. It blended with the scent of Jason's aftershave. No fruity fragrance for him. It was manly, and it reminded her of warm leather and the woods.

Jason nestled her in his arms, on the side away from his shoulder holster and weapon. Her aqua-colored silk top and pants whispered against his T-shirt and jeans. What a contrast. Her, wearing silk, mainly because that was the primary fabric in her wardrobe.

Jason, wearing jeans, snakeskin boots and a plain black T-shirt. She was betting he had a lot of those items in his closet. But that wasn't a criticism. He looked darn good. In fact, his firm, nicely shaped butt was meant for jeans, and she wasn't exactly pleased that she'd noticed that about him.

"Sorry," Jason mumbled when his arm swiped across her breast. He eased her onto the front passenger seat.

After all the inappropriate thoughts she'd had about his butt, Lilly pretended not to notice the intimate contact, even though she did suck in her breath. Thankfully, Jason pretended not to notice that.

She sighed.

This protective custody wasn't off to a good start. Lilly wasn't counting on it to get much better, either. All she could hope for was that the person who'd tried to kill her would be caught quickly so that neither Megan nor she would be in danger. As long as this person was out there, the sleeplessness would continue. So would the sickening, ominous feeling that the next breath she took could be her last. Hardly the beginning of a new life that she'd wanted when she'd first awakened from the coma.

Jason got in the SUV, started the engine and drove away from the hospital. Lilly spared the place a glance in the side mirror. She wouldn't miss it. She was anxious to get on with her life, and that getting on with it started now. Of course, she would have to return every other day for physical therapy, but that wouldn't take too much time from her plans to bond with Megan. She'd missed so much already, and she didn't intend to waste even a minute more.

"What kind of security measures have you taken to make sure all of us are safe?" she asked Jason. And by "all of us," she definitely meant Megan.

"I'm taking lots of precautions." He hitched his thumb in the direction behind them. "That's an unmarked car with two officers inside."

She took another glance in the mirror and saw both the vehicle and the plainclothes cops.

"They'll make sure no one's following us and that we get to my place in one piece," Jason explained. "I also created a little diversion by telling the hospital staff and your secretary, Corinne, that you'd be going to *your* house for a few days. There's a decoy car headed there now. It'll pull into your garage, and the officers will exit through the back. So if anyone's looking for you, they won't know if you're there or not."

All in all, it was a good plan. Or rather, it was a start to a good plan. "That's one base covered. How about your house? Is it safe?"

"As safe as I can possibly make it. It's in a gated community, and I had a new security system installed. A patrol car will make spot checks at least every hour. Of course, I'll be there, too."

Of course.

Lilly forced herself to relax and to focus on the positive. "Hey, maybe with all this protection and safeguards, the guy who tried to kill me will decide it's too big of a risk to come after me again. Maybe he'll just disappear."

"Maybe," Jason mumbled.

She noted his tight jaw and the tenseness around his eyes. "You don't believe that, do you?"

"No," he readily admitted.

Neither did she.

That's why Lilly welcomed those security measures. And she even welcomed Jason.

Because as difficult as this arrangement would be, it would be unbearable if her daughter was in any more danger than she perhaps already was. With all of Jason's faults, it seemed as if he genuinely loved Megan. Which meant he'd protect her with his life.

Lilly was counting heavily on that.

"So, it'll be Megan, you, the nanny and me staying at the house?" Lilly paused. "Or is the nanny there only during the day?"

"The nanny's name is Erica," Jason explained. "She's a live-in."

There was something in the way he offered that information that had Lilly picking through it to see if there was any hidden meaning. Her brain was obviously a little overactive because she immediately came up with a possible scenario.

"Erica's been with you since Megan was born?" she asked.

"Yes."

Okay. That didn't confirm her scenario that Erica might be more than a nanny, but again, Lilly was sure there was something left unsaid.

"Is—"

"Erica can be...a little possessive sometimes," Jason volunteered, interrupting her, which was a good thing since Lilly didn't know how she would finish that question anyway. *Are you sleeping with the nanny?* hardly seemed appropriate.

"She's possessive about Megan?"

That earned her a semiglare. "Yeah. Who else?"

"You, perhaps?"

Jason reacted as if he'd tasted something disgusting. "Not a chance."

All right. So, she wasn't stepping into a love nest/wannabe family situation, and that made her feel far better than it should have. However, the "possessive" description bothered her. After all, Jason seemed possessive. Lilly felt that way herself.

One house.

Three possessive people.

This was going to be one heck of a long stay in protective custody.

"I'm making arrangements for a nurse to come to the house," Jason continued a moment later. "But it'll take a couple of days to do a thorough security check. In the meantime, if you need help, just let me know."

There it was again. That niggling feeling that he'd left something out of his comment. "Help?" she repeated.

"Help," he verified, though he did pause after his quick response. "You know, what with the wheelchair. You, uh, might need assistance…getting around or dressing. If you do, just let me know."

She'd rather set her hair on fire.

This situation would be tense enough without him helping her in that kind of personal way.

Jason shook his head. "I don't know why I said that."

Lilly knew why. It was the same reason she'd had images of his butt and Jason and Erica in a lovers' romp. "I think it's about what happened two nights ago at St. Joseph's. That hug," she clarified when he aimed a questioning glance in her direction.

"What about it?" Judging from his stiff tone, he didn't want to discuss it any more than she did, but Lilly couldn't let this linger between them. If they were to share a house, it might be best to start with a little air-clearing.

"I don't think it was a valid attraction or anything," she concluded.

Valid? Valid! Sheez. It was a word she'd use in a corporate briefing, not in a personal discussion about inappropriate hospital embraces.

He sat there. Waiting, or something. He obviously had no plans to cooperate with the air-clearing or to question her bizarre word usage.

Lilly gave it one more try. "I think the hug and our reaction to it was some kind of, uh, knight-in-shining-armor response. You know, because you'd saved my life."

Jason shifted in his seat. "It was a hug. That's all. It can't undo what's between us."

"True." Lilly added a silent *whew* to that. She couldn't cope with hugs and possible attractions that didn't make sense.

And nothing about being attracted to Jason made sense.

She needed to concentrate on her daughter. On how she was going to deal with this first visit. On how she was going to make a place for herself in Megan's life.

And that's exactly what she did.

Lilly glanced down at the photo again. The butterflies returned with a vengeance. And the doubts. So many doubts. Including the tsunami of all doubts: Whether or not she'd be a good mother.

Before the accident and the coma, she'd spent months trying to clean up the investment business that she had inherited from her father, and she'd put the notion of children and marriage on the back burner. Of course, her experience with Greg had contributed to that back-burner decision. Talk about taking an emotional toll. Yet, if she hadn't had that brief tumultuous relationship with Greg, there would have been no Megan.

Strange that the night she'd regretted most had produced a child that she could never regret.

With that, the memories came. Good mixed with the bad. It was always that way with Greg. The night that she'd had sex with him, he'd just had a huge business setback that would almost certainly lead to bankruptcy. After drinking, he'd shown up at her house. She'd tried to console him and they'd landed in bed. Lilly had immediately realized it as a mistake since she hadn't loved him and because he'd wanted more than friendship from her.

A lot more.

Greg wanted a wedding ring and the white-picket-fence fairy tale. Unfortunately she'd told him that she wasn't ready for those things. And might never be. Angry with her rejection, he'd stormed out and minutes later was involved in a fatal car accident.

It had only been the beginning of the nightmare.

Jason had blamed her for his brother's death, and there was indeed blame to place in her lap. She'd gotten so caught up in her argument with Greg that she hadn't noticed that he was too drunk to drive.

A fatal mistake.

One she'd have to live with.

Megan didn't soften that mistake. Far from it. Because even though at the time Lilly hadn't known that they'd created a child, she'd essentially let her baby's father walk out the door and die.

"Nervous?" she heard Jason ask.

That one word pulled her out of that mixed bag of memories, and she glanced around to see what had prompted his question. With one hand, she had a death grip on Megan's picture, and with her other hand, she was choking the strap of her seat belt.

She slipped Megan's picture into her pocket. "The truth? I'm terrified."

That terror went up a notch when he took the turn into the Redland Oaks neighborhood. She'd learned from one of the cops who'd guarded her for the past two days that Jason had bought a house in the northeast area shortly after Megan was born.

"Don't expect too much for your first visit," Jason warned. He stopped at the security gate, entered his code, and the long metal arm lifted so he could drive inside. He waved at the officers in the car behind them, and the driver circled around to leave. "Megan's going through this stage where she's a little wary of people that she doesn't know. I've told her about you, but she's too young to understand."

Well, she certainly qualified as people her daughter didn't know. Lilly prayed there wouldn't be tears—from either Megan or her.

To calm her quickly unraveling nerves, Lilly forced herself to concentrate on gathering information. After all, she hadn't had much of a chance to talk with Jason about Megan. For the past two days, he'd been tied up with the investigation and security arrangements. They'd only spoken briefly on the phone, and that was only so that Jason could tell her when he'd be arriving to pick her up from the hospital. The call had lasted less than a minute.

"Can Megan walk yet?" she asked.

"More or less. She still takes a few spills, but she gets better at it every day."

Lilly had no idea if that was in the normal range of development, and she made a mental note to read some parenting books. "How about talking? Does she say anything?"

Dead silence.

Not good, considering it was a relatively easy question.

"She babbles a lot and says bye-bye and... da-da," Jason finally answered. He gave her a hard glance. "Let's just get down to the bottom line here. I love Megan. She loves me. And she calls me da-da because I'm the only father she's ever known."

Lilly couldn't dispute that, but she could take issue with what he *wasn't* saying. Suddenly this was no longer a conversation about child development. It was a conversation about all that air they hadn't managed to clear yet. "I'm her mother."

"That doesn't void the last eleven and a half months." He cursed under his breath. "Look, what happened to you wasn't your fault. I know that. But I also know I'm not just going to give Megan up now that you're out of the coma."

There it was. The real bottom line. The one they'd been tiptoeing around since the moment he'd walked into her hospital room and told her about her daughter.

Lilly shook her head. "I'm not going to give her up, either, Jason."

That hard look he was giving her got a lot harder. "Then I guess we're at a stalemate."

Not really. Yes, Jason had legal custody, but he'd gotten that custody only because she hadn't been able to care for her daughter.

Now, that had all changed.

Well, sort of.

Lilly gave herself an internal hard look similar to one she'd gotten from Jason, and she realized that their stalemate would soon turn into a huge problem. First of all, she wasn't even sure she could totally revoke Jason's custodial rights. Not without a long legal battle, anyway. During that time, her daughter would be pulled between the two of them.

But what was the alternative?

Shared custody?

Lilly could barely contain a laugh. The idea of Jason and her amicably sharing a child for, well, the rest of their lives seemed impossible. Heck, despite the danger and that now-infamous hug, they couldn't stop snipping at each other for a fifteen-minute ride.

Yes, indeed. A huge problem.

Jason pulled into the driveway of a single-story, red-brick house with smoke-gray shutters. Modest, but pristine. Very much a family house in a family neighborhood. Unlike his former place in a singles-only apartment complex. He hadn't lived there because he was a player, either. She remembered Greg explaining that with Jason's shift work and late-night undercover duties, he preferred not to live next to families with children.

Times had certainly changed.

Lilly did a quick check in the vanity mirror on the visor to see if she looked as windblown as she felt. She did. Of course, it was hard to tell with her choppy hair gathered up into a ponytail. She wasn't a vain person, but once things settled down, she'd be making an appointment with her hairdresser.

Jason got out, retrieved her wheelchair. She considered trying to walk on her own. *Briefly* considered it. But then decided that falling flat on her butt wouldn't make a good impression on Megan or the nanny. So Lilly didn't make even a grumble of a protest when Jason scooped her up into his arms and deposited her in the wheelchair.

"You're angry," she said, noting his expression.

"You're right."

Well, that anger would likely increase a hundredfold once she informed him about the discussion she'd had that morning with her attorney. Lilly was dreading what Jason and she would say to each other once he knew. And unfortunately, she would have to tell him soon—after she met her daughter.

She placed her hands on the wheels, but Jason took over that task, as well. Again, no protest from her. During the past two days she'd discovered she was lousy at steering the chair, too. Besides, he could get her there faster, and speed suddenly seemed to be a critical issue. She didn't want to wait even a second longer to see Megan.

He pushed her up the flagstone walkway lined with Mexican heather. Actual flowers. Yep. She really was going to have to adjust the old mental image she had of Jason. She'd only known him as the brooding loner, rebel-with-a-cause for justice, who was married to the badge. This wasn't the residence of a married-to-the-badge workaholic.

This was a home.

A home that Jason had created because of Megan.

That put a rather large knot in the pit of her stomach. This wasn't a competition between Jason and her, but it sure felt like one.

And he clearly had the advantage.

All the vanilla-white plantation blinds in the front window were closed. Probably a security precaution. Lilly half expected the richly stained wooden front door to open to reveal Erica and Megan standing there, ready to greet her. That didn't happen. Not only didn't the door open, it was double locked. Jason used his key so they could go inside.

The security system immediately kicked in with a buzzing sound, and he entered the code on the keypad near the door to stop the alarm from engaging. With each of these mundane, necessary actions, her heart beat even faster.

He pushed her wheelchair into the foyer. "Erica?" he called.

Nothing. No response whatsoever. And for one brief, terrifying moment, Lilly considered that the *possessive* nanny had nabbed Megan and gone on the run rather than risk losing the child. But then she heard the sound. Or rather, she heard the three sounds that happened simultaneously. Jason's cell phone rang, and there was a little high-pitched squeak, followed by a shuffle of movement.

Footsteps.

And there she was. The little girl responsible for the millions of butterflies in Lilly's stomach.

Megan Maria Lawrence.

Her daughter came barreling out of the room to the right of the foyer. Not a steady barreling, either. Every step seemed awkward and off balance, but somehow, amazingly, she stayed on her feet and didn't come to a stop until her gaze landed on Lilly.

Apparently sizing her up, Megan stood there dressed in pink overalls and a white cotton shirt with soft eyelet lace on the collar. Her auburn curls danced around her face.

Lilly's heart went into overdrive. One look, and the love for her daughter was instant. All-consuming. And in that moment, she knew she would do whatever it took to protect, to love, to keep her.

Behind her, Lilly could hear Jason talking on the phone, but the conversation didn't register. Nothing registered except Megan. Well, nothing until a woman peered out from the room Megan had just exited.

Erica, no doubt.

No all-consuming love here. No sizing up, either. The tall, leggy brunette in the breezy khaki capris and waist-length coral T-shirt had obviously already done her sizing up. With one indifferent glance from her crystal-blue eyes, she made Lilly feel like an intruder.

"Ms. Nelson," she greeted.

Lilly settled for a polite nod and returned her attention to her daughter. Megan, however, seemed far more interested in the wheelchair than the woman sitting it in. It was no doubt Megan's curiosity that had her toddling toward Lilly and the chair.

Megan aimed her index finger at one of the wheels and babbled something incoherent. But her curiosity only lasted a few seconds before she looked at Jason.

The little girl smiled.

And the smile made it all the way to those sparkling pearl-gray eyes.

The wheelchair no longer held Megan's attention, so Lilly latched on to the chair arms and forced herself to stand. That still didn't garner Megan's attention.

With that same awkward gait, Megan made her way past Lilly and to Jason. Only then did Lilly realize that he'd finished his call and was putting his phone back in his pocket. He leaned down and scooped Megan up in his arms.

"Da-da," she said.

And there was nothing incoherent about it. The little girl gave an awkward, backhanded wave and placed a kiss on Jason's cheek.

The moment was pure magic.

Lilly could almost feel her heart breaking.

Sweet heaven. Before she'd seen Megan, before she'd seen this, she'd been so certain about barging her way into Megan's life, but that kiss and smile put a huge dent in her resolve. Jason was Megan's father in every way that mattered.

Jason's gaze met Lilly's, and she braced herself for the I-told-you-so smugness that she thought she might see there. But there was no smugness. No triumphant look of any kind.

But there was concern.

"Take Megan and go to the playroom," he told Erica. "We'll be there in a few minutes."

Oh, no. This couldn't be good. Maybe now she'd get that victory speech or else a lecture on the house rules, which she'd probably already violated. Lilly eased back down into her chair and waited.

"There's something important I need to tell you," Erica said to Jason. And then she fired a narrowed-eyed glare at Lilly.

A double *Oh, no.* Erica was probably ready to voice her objection to the protective-custody arrangement.

"It'll have to wait," Jason told Erica, his insistence sounding very much like an order. He looked at Lilly. Specifically, at the chair.

Then he glanced at the room at the end of the hall. "That wheelchair will never fit through the door. You'd be stuck in the hall. Out in the open. That's too big of a risk."

"A risk for what?" Lilly asked, already knowing she wouldn't like the answer.

But Jason didn't confirm that answer, and he seemed to have a quick debate with himself before turning back to Erica. "Go ahead and take Megan to the playroom. And don't go near the windows. In fact, take her into the storage closet."

Now, that *was* an order. Just like that, Lilly's heart raced even harder and the blood rushed to her head. Whatever had caused that urgency in his voice, it wasn't a lecture about house rules.

Something was terribly wrong.

Erica must have decided the same thing. She took Megan, though the little girl protested a bit with more of those babbled syllables. Again, it was nothing coherent, but she voiced her displeasure with her adamant tone and by grabbing for Jason. However, Megan ended up grasping at the air because Erica complied with Jason's request and hurried the child out of the room.

"What happened?" Lilly asked.

Jason drew his gun from the shoulder holster. In the same motion, he grabbed her wheelchair and moved her out of the foyer. Away from the front door. He directed her into the adjacent living room, then hurried to the window. He lifted the blinds just a fraction and peeked out.

"That call was the security company that monitors the control panel at the gate," Jason offered. "They've already phoned for police backup because someone's trying to override the system."

It was difficult to hear him with her heartbeat crashing in her ears. "What does that mean?" Lilly waited, holding her breath. Praying.

"It means whoever tried to kill you is probably on the way here."

Chapter Six

Jason hadn't thought this day could possibly get any harder.

But he was obviously wrong.

He glanced at Lilly. She'd gone pale and had flattened her hand over her chest as if to try to steady her heart. Her lips were so tightly pinched together, they were practically white.

"Can you get out of the wheelchair and onto the floor?" he asked.

She gave a choppy nod and, hoping she could do it on her own, he immediately turned his attention back to the window. Or rather, back to the street that fronted the house. There wasn't a moving car in sight, but he couldn't count on it staying that way. If this was the latest attempt by the would-be killer and he or she could somehow bypass the security code, then they were all in danger.

Behind him, he heard Lilly maneuver herself out of the chair. He wished like the devil that he'd had time to carry her to the storage closet—aka the panic room—that he'd modified in case of a situation just like this one. But he couldn't take the risk of leaving the front of the house unguarded. That kind of move could put Megan in too much danger. And he was certain Lilly would agree with his decision. Megan had to come first.

"Will Megan be okay?" Lilly asked.

"Of course." Jason prayed that was true. He'd considered that the perp would figure out where they were, but he'd honestly believed that the guy wouldn't make an attempt in broad daylight to come after Lilly. He had also believed his security measures would be enough.

They *had* to be enough.

Because the alternative was unthinkable.

"What about surveillance cameras?" Lilly asked. Her voice was shaking. "Is there one at the gate?"

"Yes." But the security company had

already told him that the vehicle had heavily tinted windows and that the driver's face was obscured. In other words, they would send the video to the crime lab for analysis, but they couldn't rely on the images to make an ID.

Hell.

Without an ID or without a face-to-face confrontation, they might not figure out who was behind this. Of course, Jason wanted to know that so he could arrest the guy. But he didn't want that info at the expense of further risking the lives of the people inside his house.

Staying by the edge of the window, he fastened his attention to the street. Still no cars. No one, in fact. That was a plus on their side. Maybe this way, no innocent bystanders would be involved.

The spring breeze wasn't cooperating. It kept stirring the thick shrubs and massive oak trees that dotted the neighborhood. Each flicker of movement, each sway of the branches, every harmless sound spiked his adrenaline and sent his gaze whipping around the visible area. Thankfully, it was only the visible area he had to be concerned with because there was no street to the back of the house. And if the person gave up trying to disarm the gate and simply climbed over it, the security company would alert him.

That thought must have tempted fate.

His phone rang, the sound slicing through the room.

Jason didn't take his eyes off the street; nor did he lower his gun. Holding his breath, he pulled out his cell phone and took the call.

"It's over," he heard the now-familiar voice of the security company employee say. "The person gave up and drove away."

Jason released his breath. "Are officers in pursuit?"

"Negative. They haven't arrived yet."

That was *not* what he wanted to hear. "Call them now. Give them a description of the vehicle." Maybe it wouldn't be too late for them to apprehend and make an arrest.

"He's gone?" Lilly asked.

"It appears that way."

Jason pushed the end button on his phone and looked back at her. She was climbing into her wheelchair. Not easily, either. It was obvious the muscles in her legs weren't anywhere close to being a hundred percent.

He considered helping her, but his instincts yelled for him to continue to keep watch.

So that's what he did.

"The cops aren't going to catch him, are they?" Lilly whispered.

"They will." Though he didn't know how he would make good on that promise. He just knew they couldn't continue to go through this.

"Is everything okay?" Erica's voice poured through the house's intercom system. Only then did Jason realize she'd probably been listening since he'd installed an intercom unit in the panic room.

"It's okay," he assured her. "But just in case, don't take Megan near the windows."

Thankfully, Erica didn't ask for a just-in-case clarification. He heard the slight click to indicate she'd turned off the intercom.

Lilly wheeled her chair closer to him. She was breathing heavily, probably from the exertion and the fear. "As long as I was in a coma, Megan was safe."

It was true, yes. But Lilly hadn't been responsible for her father's business practices or her coma.

Or her recovery.

Jason was about to remind her of that when he caught the movement in the foyer. Erica. With Megan straddled on her hip, she came to the entryway of the living room. Staying away from the windows, she snagged Jason's gaze.

"Ms. Nelson's right," Erica concluded. "Megan is in danger as long as she's here."

He considered reminding Erica that it was his job to protect *both* Lilly and Megan. But it was more than that. Now that Lilly was out of the coma, Megan wasn't safe. Period. Because anyone who would attempt to murder a woman in a hospital bed probably wouldn't hesitate to use a child if it meant that child could lead him or her to Lilly.

"I have my orders," Jason explained to her, trying to keep the emotion out of his voice. It was for Megan's sake. Even though she was a baby, she could no doubt sense the tension. He hated seeing that puzzled look on her face. "And those orders are for me to protect Lilly and Megan. That's what I'll do."

Erica didn't do an eye roll, but it was close. "There's something I have to tell you," she insisted.

"Unless it's an emergency, it'll have to

wait." Jason motioned toward the playroom. "I want Megan and you in the panic room awhile longer. Until we're sure this guy isn't going to try to make a return visit."

A god-awful thought.

"It's not an emergency," Erica continued. "But it's important. I don't think it should wait. Once you've heard what I have to say, you might change your mind about guarding Ms. Nelson."

He was both intrigued and baffled by that, but Jason didn't miss the catty tone in Erica's voice. He wasn't stupid or blind. He knew that Erica had feelings for him. Despite his earlier denial to Lilly that Erica's possessiveness was limited to Megan, he knew otherwise. Oh, yes. He'd seen that *look* in Erica's eyes, and he suspected that she would like to marry him so the three of them could be a family.

That wasn't going to happen.

He has no plan for marriage. Not to Erica. Not to anyone. He needed to concentrate on two things: raising Megan and doing his job. He didn't have the time or energy for anything else. And in this case, doing his job meant dealing with Lilly and all the danger that came with her.

Lilly got her wheelchair moving in the direction of the playroom. "I'd be interested in hearing what you have to tell Jason," she said to Erica.

"You already know," Erica snapped.

She brought the wheelchair to a dead stop. Right in front of Megan and Erica. Lilly stared up at the other woman and shook her head. But then, the head shaking came to an abrupt stop, as well.

Lilly whirled the chair around so that she was facing him, but she didn't get a chance to say anything.

Erica beat her to it.

"There was a call earlier, just before you arrived," Erica said. "It was from Michael."

Michael. Erica's brother. And Jason's friend and attorney, as well. In fact, it was Michael who'd asked Jason to hire Erica to be Megan's nanny. "What did he want?" Jason asked.

"I knew something was wrong when he called," Erica explained. She was nervous now. "I pressed him to tell me. And he did because he didn't want to be blindsided by this."

"Blindsided?" Jason repeated. "By what?"

"Michael got a call from Ms. Nelson's attorney."

"Oh, my God," Lilly mumbled.

Judging from Lilly's reaction, this would be yet more bad news. Jason wasn't sure he was ready for that, but it didn't stop Erica from continuing.

"Michael said Ms. Nelson started the paperwork to revoke your custody of Megan."

OH, THIS WAS GOING to get messy.

Lilly had known this moment would come, of course, but what she hadn't counted on was having to deal with it only minutes after the scare with the possible breach of security. Judging from the fierce look that Jason was giving her, dealing with the killer or security issues might be easier than the conversation they were about to have.

"I'm sorry," Lilly said. She was. Genuinely sorry. "I intended to tell you."

His left eyebrow shot up and he indicated an un-spoken *When?* However, Jason didn't voice that question. "I want the three of you to go to the back of the house. If I need you to move into the panic room, I'll let you know through the intercom." He turned his gaze on the nanny. "Erica, Lilly will probably need help getting out of that wheelchair and into the room."

Okay. So, he didn't intend to let her explain. Not that she needed to shed much light on her decision, anyway. Since there was nothing Lilly could say to him to make this better, she decided to comply. Besides, Jason was right: it'd be safer for them to be out of the front room. Because if the would-be killer returned…

But she stopped.

Best not to go there.

Keeping a firm grip on Megan, Erica turned and headed down the hall. Lilly did the same. Not easily. The carpeted floor wasn't exactly a good surface for the wheelchair to maneuver on. Still, Lilly had no intention of asking for help.

Erica disappeared into a room at the end of the hall. Lilly tried to follow her, but it only took one hard bop of her wheels on the door frame before she realized that Jason was right—she wouldn't be able to squeeze through.

So Lilly sat there.

Like the rest of the house, the playroom reflected the same homey environment that Jason had created for Megan. Cheery pastel-yellow walls. Overstuffed floral chairs. And toys. Lots and lots of toys. Not gender-specific, either. Megan had a pinto rocking horse, dozens of colorful plastic building blocks and stuffed animals. Some of them were huge, including the fuzzy orange elephant perched in the corner near the doorway to what was probably the panic room.

"Do you need help?" Erica asked.

Yes. But Lilly wasn't going to ask for it. "I'll be fine right here."

She hoped.

The front door was only about thirty feet away. Too close if someone came barging through it. Of course, Jason wouldn't let that happen. Which only contributed to the massive amount of guilt that Lilly was suddenly feeling. She hadn't done anything wrong by trying to get custody of her daughter, but then she hadn't done it the right way, either. Despite the investigation and security arrangements, she should have found the time to tell Jason.

Megan began to squirm to get down, and Erica eased her into a standing position on the floor. Lilly almost reached out her arms—an automatic gesture to welcome Megan to come closer—but she held back, hoping the child would come to her.

She did.

Megan toddled her way and gave the wheels a cursory inspection before turning her attention to Lilly. She cocked her head to the side, a gesture that so reminded Lilly of Jason. That was his expression. Along with his eyes, Megan looked very much like his biological daughter.

"Da-da?" Megan babbled, and she yawned, rubbed her eyes and pointed to the door.

"Da-da's busy right now," Erica responded, her voice strained yet somehow soothing. "He'll be here soon." Erica sank down into a rocking chair and tipped her eyes to the ceiling before her gaze came back to Lilly. "Jason had to know about that call from your lawyer."

"Yes." It was too bad, though, that the news hadn't come from her.

But Lilly immediately rethought that. That wasn't the sort of news that could be softened, so it probably didn't matter who the messenger was. Besides, she had to give

Erica the benefit of the doubt here. The woman obviously loved Megan. If Jason lost custody, that would mean Erica would lose Megan, too. She wouldn't have any rights to see the child, either. Lilly understood that concern.

That fear.

Because even though she'd only known Megan for a few precious minutes, she couldn't imagine losing her.

Megan rubbed her eyes again, and while keeping a precarious balance, she stooped to retrieve a well-worn, blue polka-dotted blanket from the floor. She shoved it against her right cheek.

"It's her nap time," Erica explained. "She still takes two a day. One short one in the morning and another longer one in the afternoon."

Lilly felt a pang of jealousy in her heart. Such basic information. But it was info she didn't know. Here was her own daughter, her own flesh and blood, and she knew so little about her.

That would change.

Erica stood and gathered Megan into her arms. Lilly started to back out of the doorway so they could get through, but Erica waved her off. "She can take her nap in here. I'm sure that's what Jason would want."

Lilly watched as the nanny pulled open one of the chairs, converting it into a small but plushy bed. Erica got on it with Megan and cuddled with her. Another pang. A huge one. Erica was doing all the things that Lilly knew she should be doing.

"The guest room's right across the hall," Erica told her. "That's where you'll be staying."

A guest. Not that Erica had needed to emphasize that. Lilly knew her place. For the moment, anyway. But she wouldn't remain a guest in her daughter's life for long.

"The door's already open," Erica added. "But if you need help getting in, just let me know." The offer had a get-lost tinge to it.

Since Megan seemed to settle right into the nap and since Lilly felt like an intruder, she turned her wheelchair around to face yet another door she couldn't enter.

"Enough of this," Lilly mumbled. She put on the brake, shoved the metal footrests to the side, grabbed on to the chair arms, stood up and took a step.

Her muscles responded. Flexed. Moved. The way they should respond. *Almost.* For several moments, she concentrated just on that. It didn't exactly feel right, but it was better than being in that chair.

She took it one small step at a time and not without support, either. Using the wall and furniture, Lilly began to make her way around the room. She was doing okay until she banged her knee into the protruding Shaker-style dresser. But she didn't let a little pain deter her. She kept moving. An inch at a time toward her goal.

And her goal was the bed.

Where she was likely to drop like a landed trout once she reached it.

The physical exertion sent beads of sweat popping out on her forehead, and she felt dizzy. She ignored both the sweat and the light-headedness and continued. If she had any hopes of taking care of her daughter, it started with her regaining her independence.

"What the heck do you think you're doing?" she heard Jason ask.

And he asked it just as she made a final, haphazard grab for the bedpost. Her reach landed short, and she off-balanced herself.

Lilly tried to grab something, anything, but it was too late. Her shoulder smacked against the bedpost, which felt as if it were made of granite.

Jason hurried across the room and got to her just in time to loop his arm around her waist. But it didn't stop her forward momentum. In fact, it threw him off balance, as well, and they both fell hard onto the bed.

Just like that, she was in Jason's arms. Touching him all over. That touching part was even more noticeable because her top shifted in the fall and her now-bare stomach slipped against his midsection.

Body met body.

Breath met breath.

So did their gazes. They met. Held. And kept holding until there was a lot of unwanted energy simmering between them.

The entire encounter was powerful because it seemed to drain her brain and her common sense. For one moment she forgot all about the bitterness, she forgot all about Greg. Heck, she forgot how to breathe. And all she could remember was that being held had never felt this right.

Which meant it was wrong.

Totally wrong.

Lilly cleared her throat, hoping it would clear her head. It didn't. Worse, Jason seemed to be having the same problems with his thought process. She pulled away from him before she said something stupid like, *kiss me.* And for some reason, she did want him to kiss her. She wanted to know how that strong, sensual mouth would taste. She wanted to know how his lips would feel against hers.

She was obviously going crazy.

"We'll blame this on adrenaline again, okay?" he said.

It wasn't a suggestion.

Lilly nodded and adjusted her top so that her stomach was covered. She also quickly changed subjects. "I guess you must be sure the bad guy isn't close or you wouldn't be here?"

"The police arrived and are patrolling the neighborhood. If he's in the area, they'll find him. If he's long gone, then they'll beef up security at the gate. Double access codes. Extra security cameras."

All of those things were good ideas, but they wouldn't find him. Lilly was certain that the guy was long gone, which left them to deal with the aftermath. Unfortunately, part of that aftermath meant she owed Jason an apology.

"I'm sorry that I didn't tell you about calling the lawyer."

Jason spared her a narrow-eyed glance. "You should be sorry."

"Well, I am."

Another glance. Followed by an angry groan. Then he stared at her. Nope. Make that a glare. "I'm really pissed off at you right now, you know that?"

"Yes." She softly explained, "But put yourself in my place and ask yourself if you wouldn't have done the same thing."

His glare didn't soften one bit. "I'm not in the mood for reasoning here, Lilly. This isn't about logic or validity. It's about the love I have for that little girl across the hall."

"It's also about the hatred you feel for me," she pointed out.

"I don't hate you."

He said it too quickly for her to believe that he'd given it any real thought. "Liar."

"I don't hate you," he insisted.

"Maybe not. But every time you look at me, you remember Greg and how I could have saved him if I'd been thinking about him instead of me."

He shrugged and propped his hands on his hips. "If you're waiting for me to deny that, I can't."

"I know you can't." Lilly considered ending this air-clearing with that acknowledgment, but they were at an impasse here, and for Megan's sake, they needed to get past it. "Because every time I look at you, I remember the accusations and the hell you put me through that night and all the weeks after it."

That was only partly true. Which made it a lie. For reasons she didn't want to explore, she no longer saw the pain of Greg's death when she looked at Jason. Instead, she saw Jason, the man. The hot cop. The person responsible for confusing her more than she could have ever imagined.

"We need to put an end to this protective custody," Lilly informed him. "We need to figure out who tried to kill me so we can all get on with our lives."

No more glaring, but there was skepticism written all over his face. "I'll listen to any ideas you have as to how we can catch this guy."

"*Any* ideas?" she questioned.

He frowned. "Within reason."

Well, that probably ruled out what she was about to say, but Lilly went with it anyway. "I'd like to go to my office and have a look around."

He was already shaking his head before she finished. "Too risky."

"Breathing is too risky," she reminded him.

Jason leaned in, violating her personal space. "But some breaths are riskier than others."

She didn't think it was intentional, but she knew from the look on his face that he was probably thinking about that near kiss.

Yes, that was indeed one risky breath.

He was so close that she could see the swirls of gray in his eyes. Too close. Yet she did nothing to move away. It was a cheap thrill, except she knew this cheap thrill would have an enormous price tag with the potential for her heart to be broken.

"Besides," he continued, leaning back out of her personal space, "anything you need from your office, I can bring it here."

"You can't bring a conditioned response to me. In other words, something there might trigger those gaps in my memory so we'll know who's trying to kill me. And if we know that, we can catch him."

He stayed quiet a moment and then shook his head again.

"It makes sense," Lilly continued so she could cut off any objection he might try to voice. "We could go to my office after hours, with a police escort and without letting anyone outside S.A.P.D. know. You could have the building and parking lot checked to make sure it's secure."

"But that still wouldn't make it safe."

"A half hour. That's all I'd need. Just enough time to try to relive what happened that night before someone tried to kill me."

Lilly geared herself up to add more to the argument, but the sound of Megan's fussing had both Jason and her turning in the direction of the empty doorway. It didn't stay empty for long. With Erica in hot pursuit, Megan came racing into the room, and the second she spotted Jason, she made a beeline for the bed.

"I'm sorry," Erica said, coming after the child. "She doesn't seem interested in taking a nap today."

Jason lifted the child onto the bed with them. "It's okay. She can stay in here for a while."

That must have met with Megan's seal of approval because she gave Jason a kiss on the tip of his nose. The little girl climbed out of Jason's lap and worked her tiny body in between Lilly and him. Erica quietly left the room.

Lilly leaned in closer, savoring the feel of Megan's soft skin. Taking in her scent. She ran her fingers through those curls. Like air and silk. It was one of those unforgettable moments in her life. A real turning point. Her first step at getting to know her daughter.

Jason touched Megan's hair, as well, and let his fingertips trail over her cheek. It was like a sedative for Megan because her eyelids immediately drifted down. It seemed as if she was interested in taking a nap, after all.

"If I forgive you," Jason whispered to Lilly, "if I forgive myself for what happened to Greg, it'll be like letting go of him."

There it was. The catch-22 that she'd been

trying to come to terms with since that night. "I understand."

"Do you?" he challenged, but he immediately waved it off. "When Greg died, I thought there was nothing more painful than losing a brother. But now I know I was wrong." He looked down at Megan and brushed a kiss on her forehead. "There are greater heartbreaks in the world."

Yes. And losing Megan was at the top of the list.

Lilly stared at her daughter, who was nestled in the crook of Jason's arm. Megan's da-da. A connection she knew she couldn't— and wouldn't—break.

So, the question was, what kind of compromise was she willing to make to be part of Megan's life? What was she willing to do so this would work? There was only one answer; she was willing to do anything.

Anything.

And that included forging a truce, a compromise and perhaps even a relationship with her enemy. With Jason. Strange. It didn't seem as distasteful as it should.

While Lilly was mulling over that contradiction, the phone next to the bed rang.

Jason gave a weary sigh, leaned over and snatched it up. "Hello?"

Lilly couldn't hear what the caller said, but whatever it was, it didn't please Jason. He jabbed the button to turn on the speakerphone function.

"What makes you think Lilly Nelson is here?" Jason asked the caller. He looked at her and mouthed two words.

Raymond Klein.

Oh, mercy. She'd had enough of an ordeal without adding this. Yet, it was an important call because, after all, Raymond Klein was on their list of suspects. Had he called to issue some warning that he was after her? Lilly wished. Because that meant they'd know he was the one behind these attempts and the cops could haul his butt in.

"Where else would she be?" was Klein's chilly response to Jason's question.

"What do you want?" Lilly demanded. That demand earned her another glare from Jason. She was getting used to those.

"The cops keep calling me and dropping by to ask questions," Klein explained, sounding as if he were glaring, too. "You've already ruined my life—"

"FYI, *you* ruined your own life by getting involved with my father. If you hadn't done that, you wouldn't have been disbarred."

"I didn't do anything wrong. Someone set me up."

It was an old song and dance. One that she didn't want to hear again.

"I won't be drawn back into this, understand?" Klein continued. "My advice? Back off because I'm a desperate man, and desperate men don't play by the rules."

His words sent a chill through her. "That sounds a little like a threat, Mr. Klein."

"Maybe because it is."

Chapter Seven

If Jason were to make a list of Dumb-Things-To-Do, this would be at the top.

With that reminder, he didn't curse. He'd already cursed himself enough. Nor did he try to talk Lilly out of leaving the downtown office building and immediately returning to his house. He knew now that he'd be wasting his breath.

Why?

Because after two days of arguing with her about this, Lilly had delivered the ultimate ultimatum—she was going to her office with or without him.

Right.

As if *without him* was an option.

Rule number one of protective custody was to protect. Plain and simple. And he couldn't protect her if she was halfway across the city in the absolute last place she should be. He couldn't stop her from leaving, either.

It'd done no good to remind her of the incident at the hospital. Or the incident with the security gate. Or Raymond Klein's threatening call. She was here, and it was up to him to make sure she stayed safe.

The elevator came to a stop, the metal doors swishing open, and Lilly and he came face-to-face with a massive hallway lined with office doors. Even though he was a cop who was trained and armed, it was unnerving to face all that space. All those doors. Where anyone, especially a killer, could be lurking.

However, Jason knew the place was probably safe. *Probably.* Two officers who were now patrolling the parking lot had gone through every office, every hall, every nook and every cranny. There was no one else in the building except for Lilly and him, and Jason intended to keep it that way. He also intended to make this a very short visit.

In addition to the thorough building check, Jason had taken every other security precaution that he could possibly take. He'd driven a circuitous route, backtracking and watching to make sure they hadn't been followed. He had also left a police guard with Megan and Erica in case the perp decided to go in that direction instead. Now, he had to hope that all those security measures were enough to counteract the uneasy feeling in the pit of his stomach.

Jason stepped out of the elevator onto the third floor, and he reached out his arm to assist her. Lilly either didn't see his gesture, or else she blew him off. Instead, she used her cane to walk.

"Walk" being a relative term.

She was still wobbly, and he figured she'd have bruises on her palm from putting so much pressure on the cane. He'd offered to help. Lots of times. But he had finally given up trying to convince her to take the slow and easy approach to her recovery. It was like talking to a brick wall.

Or to himself.

That thought caused him to smile. God knows why. He certainly didn't have anything to smile about. He could blame that on the below-the-waist, brainless part of his anatomy. It was a myth that men were ruled by their heads and not their hearts.

Heads and hearts indeed. Those parts were

definitely involved in the process, but he knew for a fact that at this stage, lust was the number one factor.

Once this was over, he really needed to make the time to be with a woman.

Of course, his body immediately reminded him that Lilly was a woman, but he told his body what it could do with that reminder.

"Don't say it," she mumbled.

Since he was still embroiled in his own borderline lecherous mental discussion, it took Jason a moment to figure out what she'd said. Good grief, had she figured out what he was thinking?

"Don't say what?" he asked cautiously.

"About this not being a good idea."

Oh, that. "It never crossed my mind."

She laughed. One short burst of sound and air to form a *Ha!* "Sarcasm. A lost art form. I'm beginning to like you, Jason, and I don't think that's a good thing."

He didn't even have to think about that one. "It isn't. And you don't like me. Not really."

Lilly made a throaty sound of disagreement. "We're back to the you-saved-my-life stuff and that's the only reason I could possibly like you?"

They could go there. Easily. But Jason was tired of the BS. Maybe if they just dealt with it, like adults, it wouldn't be an issue.

Okay, that didn't make sense.

But avoiding it wasn't working, either.

Nothing was working.

And he'd never been more frustrated and confused in his entire life.

So, he came to a stop. Lilly stopped, too. But in the wrong place. Right in front of an open office door that had a huge window. The overhead lights created a golden spotlight above her. In fact, the light was the same color as the sleeveless top and slim short skirt she was wearing. Both silk.

How did he know that?

He'd brushed against both the fabric and her at least a dozen times. Accidentally, of course. But those inadvertent caresses still had an effect on him. A woman wearing silk. Maybe that was any man's fantasy. Judging from his reaction, it was apparently his.

Jason caught her arm and moved her to the side, away from the direct line of sight of the window, but the light still shone on her face.

Man, she was beautiful.

Not beautiful in that beauty queen,

polished sort of way. But in a natural way that stirred parts of him best left alone.

She hadn't pulled her hair into a ponytail tonight, and it instead lay against the tops of her shoulders. Those dark auburn locks were a stark contrast against the much lighter fabric of her clothes. Earrings, thin threads of gold, dangled from her ears. Jason noticed it all. Even the delicate heart necklace that lay between her breasts.

Yep, he noticed her breasts, too.

And every inch of him started to ache.

"I can't believe this is happening," he mumbled to himself. Regrettably, he didn't mumble it softly enough because Lilly's gaze whipped to his.

She stared at him, and stared. Her expression went from concern, to alarm, to disgust. Jason was sure his expression went through a similar transformation and settled heavily on the disgust part. Not disgust for her, but for himself.

"Sheez Louise. What's wrong with us?" Lilly whispered. She groaned softly. He found that erotic, too. Heck, at this point, her breathing seemed like an aphrodisiac. "And don't you dare blame it on adrenaline."

Nope, it wasn't adrenaline.

It was stupidity.

Stupidity generated by the brainless part of him that kept making really bad suggestions as to what he should do about this unexplainable attraction he had for Lilly. An attraction for his brother's lover.

Ah, there it was.

The metaphorical chastity belt. Lilly was hands-off because she was Greg's. It didn't matter that Greg was no longer alive. Just the fact that she'd slept with him—and no doubt even loved him—meant there could never be anything more than lust between them. And he had no intentions of doing anything about it.

Unfortunately, good intentions didn't always win.

"I'm attracted to you," he admitted. He heard his words and practically winced. Never, never, never did he think he'd say that to Lilly Nelson. But then, never did he think he'd want a woman this much.

She raked her finger over her jaw and shifted her posture slightly. "I'm attracted to you, too."

This time, he did wince. "You weren't

supposed to say that. You were supposed to slap me or something."

Lilly lifted an eyebrow. Paused. Stared. "Trust me, Jason, over the past few days there are a lot of things I've thought about doing to you…" Her voice changed. The air changed. He changed. Everything changed. "But slapping you isn't one of them."

Oh. Hell.

"That was the wrong thing to say." Jason was surprised he could manage something as complex as human speech. His body and energy were suddenly pinpointed on only one thing.

Kissing Lilly.

"Anything I could say, or didn't say, would have been wrong." Lilly shrugged. "Or right. Depending on your perspective."

His perspective apparently wasn't that good right now. Neither was hers. He was sure of it.

"I blame it in part on your jeans," she informed him.

Even with their no-holds-barred conversation, he hadn't expected her to say that. "Excuse me?"

"Your jeans," Lilly said as if that clarified

everything. She waited a moment. "You look really good in them. You look really good, period. And maybe because it's been so long since I've had sex. Or maybe it's you. Or me. Or the moonlight. Or your aftershave. Or maybe it's because I'm just going crazy."

Well, they were definitely on the same wavelength, and it wasn't a good place to be. "My aftershave, huh?" Jason questioned.

She nodded. "It reminds me of leather and sex."

He frowned. "And that's a good thing?"

"Apparently so." She touched his arm, rubbed softly. Stopped. Then started again. Her fingers moved to the front of his white cotton shirt. To his chest. And she began to play with the fabric. "When I was in the laundry room this morning, I sniffed your T-shirt." She huffed. "See what you've reduced me to? Clothes sniffing. Thanks to you, I'm now a bona fide pervert."

Lilly had no doubt meant that to make him laugh. Or at least she'd meant it to break the almost unbearable tension. It didn't work. No amount of humor or sarcasm was going to defuse this.

He didn't move.

Neither did Lilly.

But he did move closer. Yep. He went in the wrong direction. His gaze traveled over her moonlit face and searched her eyes. He saw a lot of concern there. Maybe even fear. And unfortunately there was something much, much worse. He saw mirrored in her what stirred his own body.

Desire.

Minutes earlier Jason had been certain that he'd filled his quota of doing stupid things. But he was apparently wrong. He saw a flash of the future and realized he was about to make the stupidest mistake of his life.

That didn't stop him.

Nothing would stop him. He knew that now. So he quit fighting.

He reached out, slid his hand around the back of Lilly's neck and hauled her to him. She made a soft gasp when she landed against his chest. Not a gasp of shock or discomfort. It was breathy. A quivery, feminine sound.

"We're practically at war with each other," she reminded him.

It was a good reminder.

And a useless one.

"That whole war thing between us…" he lowered his mouth to hers "…is cooling down a bit." He brushed his lips over hers and elicited another of those gasps from her. "Wouldn't you say?"

"It's a little cool. But still there. And that means we shouldn't kiss," she said, her breath clipped. She shook her head and the movement stirred her hair around her face, the wisps landing on her cheek.

"Well, we have to start somewhere. It would hardly seem appropriate if we had sex without kissing first."

Now, she laughed. It was low, rich and filled with nerves. Jason knew how she felt. Every nerve in his body was on edge.

Her scent curled around him, blending with those of the cool, damp air-conditioning and the spring night. There were undertones of her arousal. Subtle. Yet not subtle to his own body. He wanted his scent on her skin. Her scent, on his. Hell, he just wanted her.

He skimmed his thumb over her bottom lip.

"Jason—"

He didn't let her finish. Fitting his mouth

to hers, he kissed her. It was quick and light.
No urgency. No demands. Almost immediately he lifted his head to gauge her reaction.
Her eyes were wide, her mouth pursed in what appeared to be surprise. Or maybe outrage. It wasn't quite the reaction he'd hoped for. He'd hoped to see a punch of lust in those ocean-colored eyes.

So, he kissed her again.

This time her breath quickened. Her clenched hand trapped between them relaxed, for just a moment, before she gripped the front of his shirt and pulled him closer.

It was the only invitation he needed.

Running his hand into her loose hair, he recaptured the back of her neck and gently angled it so he could deepen the kiss. She made a little sound, just enough to part her lips. Enough for him to slip past the sweet barrier of her lips and discover plenty about Lilly Nelson.

LILLY HAD BEEN so sure that Jason would taste like a combination of mint and ice. But there was nothing cool and minty about him. He was all fiery hot, as was the possessive grip he had around the back of her neck.

She didn't fight the kiss, the grip, him or anything else. The only fight she had was to get closer to him. Jason did the same. Fighting and grappling, they came together, and she felt the solid muscles of his chest. Felt the sinewy strength of his arms. And with all that feeling, the kiss continued.

Jason escalated things. If he hadn't, she would have. The kiss was already French and immensely pleasurable, but he used that clever mouth to make her want more.

He was aroused. Lilly felt his erection brush against her stomach. She wanted to feel even more of it, but she braced her hand on his chest to stop herself from doing that. It would be wrong to touch him, to move against him.

But it would feel darn good. She was sure of it.

His kiss had created a fire inside her. An ache. And that ache was already demanding relief.

Her hand on his chest must have caused him to stop, because Jason tore his mouth from hers and looked down at her. Judging from the just-kill-me-now expression, he'd come to his senses and wasn't pleased about this momentary surrender to passion. She hadn't come to her senses yet, but Lilly knew she'd have to, soon. Having sex against the wall probably wasn't a good idea.

Probably.

Even if it suddenly seemed like the best idea in the world.

"You're a good kisser," she confessed. His breath gusted against her face. "I'd hoped you wouldn't be."

His breath continued to gust, and he sounded as if he'd just run a marathon. "Then we're even. I'd hoped you wouldn't be, either. It would have put an end to this in a hurry."

"All right. The kiss doesn't have to mean anything. In fact, I insist that it not mean anything."

He nodded. "So do I."

"Good. We're in agreement. Maybe a first for us."

But agreeing didn't make it so. Lilly knew that kiss meant *something*. She could already feel the difference between them, and it wasn't just about heavy breathing, racing pulses and the most primitive of urges. There were now huge dents in those barriers between them. But maybe, just maybe, they wouldn't be adding any more dents in the near future.

"We have a lot of things to work out," Lilly reminded him. And while she was at it, she reminded herself.

He considered that a moment. Nodded again. But what was missing was the part about him truly believing that the kiss didn't matter, that it meant nothing. She could see his skepticism written all over his face.

"We won't even discuss it again," she continued, hating that she'd become a motor-mouth, hating even more that Jason wasn't offering a thing to explain all of this away. Heck, she shouldn't be the only one tripping over her tongue. "We'll concentrate on the case, on getting the files and getting out of here."

There. Finally, she saw it. The slow, necessary transformation from hot kisser to hot cop. Correction: hot, dedicated cop. Which was exactly the persona she needed with her tonight. The reminder had worked. Jason no doubt remembered the danger, the person who wanted her death and the seriousness of their situation.

Good.

At least one of them now had the right mind-set.

Before she could do anything else stupid, Lilly moved away from him, something she should have done before they'd started their little verbal foreplay that'd led to that kiss. And she moved quickly. Well, as quickly as her impaired legs would allow. She went down the hall to her office.

Jason stepped in front of her and did his cop thing by surveying the place. He then stepped to the side. What he didn't do was say a word. Or look at her. He kept his attention on the room itself.

Oh, yeah. They'd really ruined things with that kiss.

"Your attorney had planned to move all your things out in five months," Jason explained, his gaze still surveilling. "Everything would have been placed in storage until Megan became an adult."

Five months. That would have been the two-year point of her coma. Lilly was a little surprised that her attorney had waited so long to do that. But maybe there'd been legal issues involved. Maybe even issues that involved declaring her dead. A thought that sent goose bumps over her skin.

She switched on one of the overhead lights and forced herself to concentrate on something other than the coma and Jason. She started with the basics and checked to see what was familiar and what wasn't. Her functional, no-fuss desk was there, as was a computer that was no doubt hopelessly out of date. Across from the desk was a trio of saddle-brown leather chairs and a small table—bare. No plants, but then they'd probably died and been removed. Other than that, everything was the same.

Well, almost.

Lilly certainly didn't feel the same. She felt like a visitor to a place where she'd once spent seventy-five percent of her time. The work had seemed so important then. Vital, even. It didn't seem that way now.

"Well?" Jason prompted, his voice tight and impatient. Probably because he was anxious to leave. "Does being here trigger any memories?"

"Only that I'd become a workaholic those weeks before the coma." Pressing her cane against the floor, she took a step inside and pulled in a deep breath. The place smelled like dust and lemon air freshener.

Probably a sicko metaphor for her life.

She went to her desk and opened the bottom file drawer. The folders were still there. Right where she'd left them. She pulled out the one that was marked Urgent and sat so she could study it. Or rather, study what was left in it. The file had once been huge, at least two inches thick, and now it contained less than a dozen pages. Someone had obviously removed the majority of the documents; after thumbing through the file, she decided the missing pages pertained to the investigation into her father's activities.

Jason turned on the computer, pulled up one of the leather chairs and got to work, as well. "Should I remind you that the police have already been through all of this?" he quipped.

"Should I remind you that people, even cops, miss really obvious things when they look for evidence?" Lilly countered.

He gave her a flat look. "There's a fine line between the lost art of sarcasm and being a smart-ass." But the corner of his mouth lifted into a semismile when he said it. A smile that warmed her in places it shouldn't have. Especially her heart.

Oh, sheez.

The man had dimples. What kind of defense could a woman have against those? Her twenty-nine-year-old brain had obviously regressed to that of a hormonally pumped teenager.

It was obviously time for a change of subject. And a change of attitude. Lilly knew just what it would take to do that. "By the way, I want to thank you for helping Megan adjust to being around me."

Just like that, Jason's semismile faded, and she watched by degrees as he closed down. Now he wasn't just a cop, but the hard-nosed officer she'd come to know. Kissing and becoming aroused were okay. Ditto for light flirting. But talking about Megan was still touchy territory. Lilly wanted it to stay that way for a while. Until she got over her lust-fest for Jason. She needed that to make sure she kept her hands, and the rest of herself, off him.

"I think Megan's getting used to me," Lilly added.

"Yes." Just a yes. It was practically a roadblock.

"Not Erica, though." Lilly tested the waters. In fact, this was the first time she'd been able to discuss Erica with Jason, since the woman always seemed to be around. "She doesn't like me."

He shook his head. "It's not that—"

"She's possessive, I know," Lilly interrupted.

"And she's jealous."

Okay, so Jason hadn't closed down as much as she thought. Nor was he oblivious or blind to Erica's feelings for him. "Just how much influence does Erica have over you?"

"What's that supposed to mean?" he snapped.

The water testing was over and she'd apparently jumped in headfirst. "Nothing sexual." Lilly knew that now that she had seen the two of them together. That didn't mean Erica was powerless in this weird quadrangle of a relationship. "It's just when the time comes to work out Megan's custody, I don't want Erica to interfere."

"She won't," he said gruffly. He didn't add more. In fact, he didn't even maintain eye contact. Instead he checked his watch. "I told the officers in the parking lot that we'd only be here an hour at the most."

In others words, cut the custody chat, the flirting and any residual lusting and get down to the business at hand. She did. Lilly skimmed over a copy of the initial report that she'd sent to the police. The report that detailed some of her father's shady dealings. There was nothing surprising about it. She remembered writing it, remembered the effect it had. In short, it had led to an investigation that had in turn led to Wayne Sandling and Raymond Klein's disbarments. She'd crossed all the t's. Dotted all the i's.

So what if anything was missing?

"Have I overlooked something so obvious that it's staring me right in the face?" she mumbled. "What if this isn't connected to my father's business?" The question was meant more for herself than Jason.

"You have another theory?" He moved closer. Probably to see what she was reading that had prompted her comment. But he also must have remembered what'd happened the last time they'd gotten close.

Jason moved back.

Lilly sighed.

"Road rage, perhaps?" she suggested. "Maybe I was in some kind of driver-to-driver altercation that night, and it turned bad."

He made a sound of disagreement. "And this person is carrying a grudge after nineteen months?"

She turned toward him and lifted her eyebrow, a reminder of the grudge he'd carried all this time.

"Sarcasm," he complained. "I've heard it's a lost art form."

Except she was no longer sure he was holding a grudge. Lilly rethought that. Or maybe that kiss was nothing more than just that—a kiss. A basic physical reaction and nothing more.

Hey, it was possible.

And what with his fatherly duties and high-pressure job, it'd probably been a while since Jason had kissed or been kissed.

He leaned closer and whispered, "Best not to think about it."

She knew what he meant. He wasn't talking about her road rage/grudge-holding theory. He was referring to *them*. And Jason was right.

"Think about Wayne Sandling and Raymond Klein," he continued.

Oh, she was thinking about them. Even the kiss couldn't diminish that. "Means, motive and opportunity. They both have that in spades. And while I know they're guilty of illegal business practices, is either of them actually guilty of wanting me dead?"

"Time will tell." He paused. "Any other names that jump out at you?"

She shook her head. "Not really. But that's what scares me. It could be some person that we don't even know about. Someone who was smart enough to keep his name from drawing attention. My father wasn't exactly discriminate about his business associates."

Jason's cell phone rang and Lilly was in such deep thought that it took her a moment to realize what it was. He snatched his phone from his pocket and answered it. And Lilly immediately became alarmed, because he'd told the two officers in the parking lot to alert him if anything went wrong.

So, had something gone wrong?

She closed the file folder and reached for her cane in case they had to dive for cover. With all the danger of the past four days, she would have thought her body had grown accustomed to the fear.

It hadn't.

Lilly reacted as if this were the first time. The racing heart. The thin breath. The sickening feeling of dread that came from having little or no control over a potentially deadly situation.

Because there was nothing else she could do, she waited, watching for any cues on Jason's face. There were emotions there, all right. Confusion. Questions. Concern. It was the concern that created all sorts of wild scenarios in her head.

"Is Megan okay?" Lilly asked the moment he took the phone away from his ear.

"This isn't about Megan. Your former secretary, Corinne, is downstairs, and she wants to see you."

Well, it wasn't the threat she'd tried to prepare herself for. "Corinne's here?" Lilly checked the time at the bottom of the computer screen. It was already past 11:00 p.m. Hardly the hour for an office visit.

"She says she was just driving by and saw the lights." Jason paused. "You want to see her?"

She almost said no, because she wanted to continue to go through the files, but there was something about Corinne's visit and her saw-the-lights explanation that piqued Lilly's curiosity.

"Sure."

Jason relayed that to the cop and ended the call. "You think Corinne knows something?" he asked.

"Probably not. If she did, she would have already given the information to the police." Still, that didn't rule out Jason's theory about Corinne having some information. Like the cops and everyone else who'd been through the files, Corinne might have missed something.

Because time was preciously short, Lilly reopened the file folder and continued to go through it while they waited for Corinne's arrival. Jason did more than wait. He put the computer on a screensaver and withdrew his weapon.

That got her attention. "You think Corinne's an assassin coming in here to finish me off?" Lilly asked, conveying her skepticism.

"I'm not taking any more chances."

Lilly was about to point out that Corinne was almost fifty. A grandmother at that. On a profiling scale, she wouldn't be in the top one hundred suspects. Still, she didn't object to Jason's diligence. It was that diligence that'd kept her alive so far. More so, she trusted him, and she swore to herself that her change of heart had nothing to do with this odd intimacy that was now between them.

She heard the elevator door open and then the footsteps. Two sets. Probably Corinne's and the police escort's. Several moments later, both appeared in the doorway.

Like her office, the changes in Corinne were minimal. A few more gray hairs threaded through the rich chestnut strands. Maybe she'd put on a pound or two. But that was it. No sinister vibes that she was a killer. Then, Lilly hadn't expected to get such vibes, anyway.

"It's so good to see you." Corinne went to her, reached out and hugged her. "How have you been?"

"Better. I think." Lilly returned the hug while staying seated. "It's good to be among the living."

Corinne pulled back and the sadness crept

into her blue eyes. "What happened to you was horrible. I still can't believe it."

Corinne glanced at Jason's unholstered gun, the file folder and finally at the computer screen that, thanks to Jason, was now spewing stars and other celestial objects. Corinne's bottom lip quivered. Not an unusual gesture. Lilly had experienced lots of Corinne's lip-quivering when they'd been embroiled in the police investigation. The woman wasn't very good at hiding her nerves.

Corinne clamped her teeth over her bottom lip to stop it from quivering and waited a moment until she'd gotten control of herself. "You think you'll be reopening the office any time soon?"

"I'm not sure," Lilly answered.

In fact, she hadn't given it much thought. What with getting acquainted with Megan and the near-smothering, Lilly was still trying to find equilibrium. According to her financials, she had more than enough money to keep the business closed for another year or two. It might take that long to resolve the custody issues and find the person who wanted to kill her. Getting back to work definitely wasn't high on her list of priorities.

"What about you?" Lilly asked. "What have you been doing for the past nineteen months?"

"Well, after I tied up some loose ends around here and after the police were finished with their search, I went to work for an investment firm over on St. Mary's. Still, I like to drop by here every now and then to check on the place."

"And you decided to check on it tonight?" Jason couldn't keep the cop out of his voice.

"Because I saw the lights on. Usually I just stop by during regular business hours because I no longer have a key to get into the building." She blew out a nervy breath and turned her attention back to Lilly. "What about you? Where are you staying now that you're out of the hospital?"

"A police safe house," Jason volunteered before Lilly could answer for herself. It wasn't exactly a lie, but it was obvious Jason didn't want Corinne to know where she was. "It has lots of security," he added. "Someone tried to hurt Lilly while she was in the hospital, and we don't want anyone coming after her again."

"I see." Corinne's breath quickened, and she made a vague motion toward the door. "Well, it's obvious you two are working, and I need to get home. So, I'll just be going."

They exchanged goodbyes. Hasty, polite ones. And Corinne headed for the door with the police guard following right along behind her.

"Do you trust her?" Jason asked.

Lilly opened her mouth to say yes, but the one-word response stuck in her throat. Yes, Corinne had been a great secretary. Loyal. Efficient. Not from Lilly's father's regime, either. Once Lilly had discovered the discrepancies and the illegal activity, she'd wiped the slate clean. All employees had been let go, and she'd started fresh with Corinne. A woman who had no ties to her father.

But that didn't mean Corinne couldn't be bought.

There were a lot of riled people who'd been burned by her father's business practices, and maybe one of those riled people now had Corinne on their payroll.

"I really don't know if I can trust her," Lilly admitted.

"Then we're not staying any longer. Let's get out of here."

Lilly didn't argue. Corinne's visit might have been legit, but it had rattled her. She grabbed the file she'd been reading and tucked it and several others beneath her arm. Jason took the remaining folders from the drawer and took her arm to get her moving.

Despite her limp and the cane, they made it out of the building in record time. Corinne was nowhere in sight, but Lilly immediately spotted the two officers in the dimly lit parking lot. One was near their vehicle, which was as close to the building as possible without parking on the sidewalk. The other cop was at the far end at the entrance. The two were definitely guarding the place as much as they could, considering the office building was sandwiched between other buildings.

And that wasn't the only security concern.

At the front of the parking lot there was a semi-deserted street. At the back stood a row of eight-foot-high blooming mountain laurels. Fragrant and beautiful. But they'd also make a great hiding place. She hoped the officers had thoroughly searched that area because Jason and she still had to make their way down a long stretch of the sidewalk.

"Keep walking," Jason insisted.

She heard the concern in his voice and realized something wasn't right.

Lilly could feel it, and it was bone deep.

A warning that speared through her until her breath was racing right along with her too-vivid imagination.

She continued walking, faster though, her cane and her flat sandals thudding like heartbeats on the pebbled concrete. She glanced over her shoulder. No one was following them. No one was lurking in those mountain laurels or in the shadows of the buildings.

So maybe she'd been wrong about things not being right.

It was, after all, coming up on midnight, the proverbial witching hour. Someone obviously wanted to kill her. That was a solid enough reason to get a case of the willies. That was probably all there was to it. A good old-fashioned case of frayed nerves and willies.

Lilly had convinced herself that all was well.

Until she heard the sound. A sort of click.

The *all's well* rationalization that she'd fought so hard to find evaporated at the exact moment that she heard another sound.

No click this time.

It was a deafening blast.

And a bullet slammed past her.

Chapter Eight

Jason didn't need anyone to tell him what that god-awful sound was. He knew. And he cursed. Because he was well aware that someone was shooting at them.

Hell.

They were still a good five or six yards from his SUV. Too far to make it in a single dive. Especially for Lilly. As a temporary measure, Jason hooked his arm around Lilly's waist and pulled her off the sidewalk and into a cluster of shrubs. She was already headed in that direction anyway so thankfully she didn't take too hard of a fall.

Another shot tore through the night and slammed into the ground. Mere inches from Lilly's head.

So much for his temporary safety measure

of being in the shrubs. To keep her alive, they'd have to move.

"Let's go," Jason ordered.

With his arm still around her, he drew his Glock and dragged Lilly out of the shrubbery and to the side of the SUV. It was safer than using the plants as a shield, but it didn't neutralize the danger, because judging from the angle of the two shots, the gunman was somewhere on a rooftop. That meant he or she was in a perfect position to adjust, re-aim and fire again.

And that's exactly what happened.

The shot skipped off the roof of his SUV, metal tearing through metal.

"Who's doing this?" Lilly mumbled. Not a question exactly. More like a furious, frustrated plea.

Jason heard the other officers scrambling for cover and position. Either or both would be able to return fire, but that didn't mean they could take out the shooter before he or she took out one of them. He moved his body over Lilly's, sheltering her as best he could, and he scanned the rooftops to see if he could catch a glimpse of the sniper.

Nothing.

For a few seconds.

The gunfire returned. Not a single shot, either. A barrage of deadly bullets that pelted the ground and the SUV. Jason felt totally helpless. All he could do was stay put and pray the shots would stop so he'd get his own opportunity to put an end to this. Unfortunately he couldn't just start firing random shots. They were literally in downtown San Antonio, and he didn't want to shoot anyone by mistake.

Beneath him, Jason could feel Lilly trembling, and he hated that once again she'd been placed in a situation where her life was at serious risk. Her question had been dead-on—*Who's doing this?* Because until he knew that, stopping it would be hit or miss.

Jason was damn tired of missing.

The shots continued for what seemed an eternity, and just like that, in the blink of an eye, they stopped.

He waited. Listened. For any sound to indicate the gunman was reloading. Or escaping. When he heard nothing other than the normal noises of the city, he turned and pinpointed the roof of the adjacent building. The spot where he believed the shots had been fired.

"Do you see him?" Lilly asked.

Because she lifted her head, Jason used his forearm to keep her down and hopefully out of harm's way. This lull could be a ploy by the gunman to get them to leave cover. He wasn't about to allow Lilly to take that risk.

"Anything?" Jason shouted to his fellow officers.

"Negative," they answered within seconds of each other.

And the silence continued. No shots. No out-of-place sounds.

Nothing.

"I've called for backup," one of the officers advised.

Good. It shouldn't take long for them to arrive, either, since they were only about three miles from headquarters. It was too bad, though, that the shooter could be long gone by then, as well.

"Keep a visual on the perimeter of that other building," Jason ordered the officers.

Because what went up had to come down, eventually. That wouldn't necessarily happen, though, at the front of the building. A more likely escape route would be the back. He considered going there, but he immediately ruled it out. The gunman was after Lilly. That didn't mean he or she wouldn't kill others to get to her, but if Jason left, Lilly would be unprotected. He could be playing right into the gunman's hands. Still, he had to do something to try to nail this guy.

While keeping a vigilant watch, Jason used his cell phone to contact one of the officers. This definitely wasn't something he wanted to shout out for the shooter to hear. "Take your partner and proceed to the back of that building where the shots originated. Try to cut off any potential escape route."

"Will do," the officer said, hanging up.

It was a huge undertaking. And probably a futile one. The building spread across nearly a third of the city block, and it would take a dozen or more cops to secure it properly. Still, it was better than nothing, and with backup on the way, they might get lucky.

Might.

"If this is about revenge," Lilly whispered, "then we're back to Wayne Sandling and Raymond Klein."

He heard a "but" at the end of Lilly's comment, and he understood it. Maybe it wasn't about revenge at all but something that Lilly knew. Or something she could learn. Possibly from those files. Or possibly something that'd been on that disk she'd planned to give to the police.

Of course, that left Jason with a huge question. If the person responsible for these latest attempts on Lilly's life had also been the one to run her off the road and steal the disk, then wasn't it finished?

Why had the attempts to kill her continued?

Either the perpetrator believed there was other incriminating information than just the one disk—info that was trapped inside Lilly's head—or, as Lilly said, it could be for revenge.

Or…

Jason almost hated to finish that thought, but he did. This could be related to none of that. But if so, then who would stand to gain something, anything, if Lilly were out of the way?

He didn't like the first thought that came to mind, but it came anyway.

Erica, maybe?

He was about to go through all the reasons

why it wasn't possible for his nanny to be guilty when his phone rang.

"Detective Lawrence," Jason answered.

"We made it to the back of the building." It was one of the officers. "But it's not good news. We saw someone speed away in a dark-colored car. The license plate was covered with mud or something."

Jason cursed. "How about a description? Were you able to get that?"

"Negative."

Not that it helped, but he cursed some more. "Find Wayne Sandling and Raymond Klein and bring them in to headquarters. *Now.* I've got questions to ask, and by God, they'd better have the answers."

LILLY COULDN'T STOP shaking.

It was as if her body had decided it'd had all it could take and it was going to punish her for the trauma. So she trembled from head to toe while she stood there, behind the interrogation mirror where the detectives had left Wayne Sandling.

Sandling certainly wasn't trembling. With his hands tucked behind his head and his legs stretched out in front of him, he practically lounged at the austere metal table, waiting for the detectives to return so they could continue the questioning. Not that the questioning was actually leading anywhere: Sandling had denied any involvement in the shooting.

Despite being called out in the middle of the night to be interrogated by police for an attempted homicide, Sandling appeared well-rested and was dressed to perfection in a flawlessly tailored business suit. He was calm and collected.

Unlike her.

"I feel like a genuine wuss," Lilly muttered.

Jason glanced at her and frowned. "Why?"

She held up her hand to show him that she was shaking.

"That makes you feel like a wuss?" he challenged. "It's a normal human response to having your life threatened."

"You're not shaking," she pointed out.

"I'm a cop. I've been trained not to shake. But if it helps, I'm shaking inside."

She didn't believe him for a minute, but yes, it did help to think that he wasn't impervious to all of this. How could murder and mayhem ever become routine for anyone, even for a cop? Lilly knew it would be a long time, if ever, before she could forget the sound of those shots. They'd gotten lucky. Any one of those bullets could have killed them.

"The incident reports are done," Jason told her. "And it doesn't appear Sandling is on the verge of a confession, so I'll make arrangements for an officer to take you back to the house, okay?"

It wasn't the first time Jason had suggested that. It was the third time in the four-plus hours they'd been at police headquarters. She wasn't any more amenable to the offer now than the first time he'd made it.

"I want to be here when Raymond Klein is questioned," Lilly reminded him.

"It might be hours before they even find him."

"Then, I'll be here for hours."

Obviously not pleased about that, Jason huffed. But the sound had barely faded when he slipped his arm around her waist. "I don't suppose you'll let me get you a chair, either?" he asked.

Ah. So the arm thing wasn't a lovey kind of gesture. It was because she probably didn't look too steady on her feet. "It's strange, but all the fear and adrenaline have made my leg muscles feel stronger. Don't worry, though. I won't be suggesting gunfire and near death as a form of treatment for rehabbing coma patients."

"More sarcasm." The corner of his mouth lifted a fraction. "You're really good under pressure, you know that?"

"Right." Just in case he'd forgotten, she gave him a repeat demo of her trembling hand.

"Proves nothing. We've already established that. And you *are* great under pressure." He stopped, mumbled something incoherent. "But then, several of my perceptions about you have changed over the past few days."

Lilly considered that. Nodded. "I could say the same for you." She considered that some more. Shook her head in disgust. "But those perceptions have changed mainly because we have the hots for each other."

Judging from the look in his eyes, he wanted to deny that. Lilly knew he couldn't. "I shouldn't have kissed you," he concluded.

Yes, that particular intimate act was the

proverbial point of no return, but she wouldn't let him shoulder the entire blame for this. "I kissed you back."

"It shouldn't have happened. I feel guilty as hell. Like I've betrayed my brother—"

"I know. I feel guilty, too." Not that it helped.

She'd known all along that Jason would see any attraction for her as the ultimate disloyalty to Greg. And there was a reason for that. Greg was…well, unrealistic when it came to her and the future he'd wanted them to have together. He certainly wouldn't have given Jason and her his blessing to jump headfirst into a relationship.

"I'll tell you what," she suggested, because they both needed an out. "Let's not kiss again, and that way we avoid this whole big guilt-fest. Agreed?"

Jason stared at her. "You think agreeing will make it happen?"

No way. But she kept that to herself. "I think we have to accept that abstinence is the way to go because we don't have time for the alternative." She tipped her head to Sandling. "We only have time for that. And by *that*, I mean I don't want us to die. I want Megan to be safe. The only way all of that can happen is for us to prove Sandling's responsible or else find the real culprit and put him or her behind bars."

It was a good speech. And it was even true. Well, for the most part. Lilly did want to keep Megan and Jason safe. She wanted the would-be killer stopped. But she didn't think all the distractions in the world would stop her from wanting the man beside her.

She'd relived that kiss a half dozen times. The taste of him. The way she'd felt when he'd held her in his arms. Everything about it was wrong, especially the timing. And yet, everything about it felt right. As long as it continued to feel right, she didn't think she had a snowball's chance in Hades of stopping what had already started.

But what exactly had started?

"Only a pathological liar could be that calm during an interrogation," she heard Jason say.

She followed his gaze, and it was fixed on Sandling and the detective who'd just reentered the room. "He probably knows we're watching him, and he wants to rile us with this iceman routine."

"Well, it's working," Jason snarled.

Yep, it was. She glared at Sandling as he gave a flippant chuckle when the detective reminded him that he had a motive for the shooting. A motive for the attempted smothering. And a motive for trying to get through the security gate in Jason's neighborhood.

That motive was *her*.

"So do a lot of other people," Sandling calmly concluded while he examined his nails. "Including, but not limited to, my former law partner, Raymond Klein. I trust you'll ask him these same boring questions?"

The detective didn't respond, and instead paraphrased a previous question about Sandling's whereabouts during the shooting. As he'd done before, Sandling denied everything. What Lilly couldn't decide—was he telling the truth? Sandling seemed a little too meticulous for what was essentially a string of incredibly non-meticulous crimes.

That didn't make him innocent.

The inconsistencies between his somewhat prissy demeanor and the crime scenes could have been intentional. A way to throw them off his trail. The tactic could stall them for weeks.

Or forever.

That created a sinking feeling in the pit of her stomach, and she groaned softly. "What are we going to do about Megan? How can we keep her safe?"

"We'll have another guard at the house starting today." Judging from his quick response, Jason had given this lots of thought. "A sort of cop-nanny. I might go ahead and try to set up a safe house. I'm not sure if it'd be any safer than a gated community, but I'm still considering it."

Lilly sorted through all that info and immediately discovered what he *hadn't* said. "What about Erica?"

"I think it might be a good idea if she isn't staying there with us any longer." He slid his arm from her waist and checked his watch. "I'll see if they've managed to locate Raymond Klein. I also need to call the crime lab to find out if they got anything from the video surveillance camera they took from the security gate."

She caught his arm to stop him from leaving. "Wait a minute. You didn't think I'd just let that part about Erica pass, did you? Why are you giving her the boot? Is it because she doesn't like me?"

"No." He hesitated and then repeated it.

"No. It's because I'm not sure I can trust her."

It was like being hit by a big sack of rocks. Trust was the issue here? Lilly hadn't seen that one coming. Jealousy, yes. Possessiveness, definitely. Too many cooks in the kitchen scenario—that, too.

But not lack of trust.

Lilly would certainly have grilled Jason until he told all about this distrust issue. She would have if there hadn't been a knock at the door. Just one sharp rap, and it opened. It was Detective O'Reilly, the officer who'd been assisting Jason on the case.

"We found Raymond Klein," O'Reilly told them. "He's being taken into interrogation now."

That got Jason moving. He stepped around O'Reilly and into the hall. Lilly followed him. Or rather, she tried to. Jason turned and tried to stop her. But that didn't work, either. Because instead of deterring her from seeing her possible attacker, Klein came straight to them.

Lilly had no trouble recognizing the man. After all, they'd run into each other plenty of times during the investigation that'd led to his disbarment.

Klein hadn't changed at all in the past nineteen months. The same slightly shabby salt-and-pepper hair. The overly round face that was cragged with too many wrinkles considering he was only in his late thirties. All those wrinkles and his heavy brow gave him a permanent sourpuss expression.

"I thought we'd settled this," Klein greeted. He looked right past Jason and O'Reilly and aimed his greeting at her.

Jason stepped protectively in front of her. Lilly huffed and tried to reestablish her ground, but Jason would have no part in that. The best she could manage was to move to Jason's side so she could face Klein head-on.

"I want him tested for GSR," Jason relayed to O'Reilly.

"Gunshot residue?" Klein supplied. "You'll need a warrant for that."

"We already have it," Jason confirmed.

Klein's chin came up. "You're wasting your time, Detective."

That was probably true. Klein's hair was still damp, indicating a recent shampoo. If he was the shooter, he'd no doubt have worn gloves, showered and changed his clothes. He wasn't the sort of man to get caught with the obvious. It'd taken her twice as long to connect Klein to her father as it had for her to do the same for Sandling. In the end, the authorities had gotten him for a suspicious report he'd made to the city engineers. A report that had ultimately allowed her father to receive a contract where he'd taken a ton of money and provided minimal services in exchange. Klein's part in that deal had been barely enough to get him disbarred.

And he wasn't about to let her forget that.

Raymond Klein hated her. Lilly had no doubts about that. But the question was, had he done something about that hatred, or was this anger simply because he felt he'd been railroaded again?

Though it seemed a senseless exercise, Lilly tried to remember what'd happened that night of her accident. Had she seen her attacker's face? Was it Klein's face? And was that the reason he now wanted her dead—because she would be able to identify him if and when her memory returned? Unfortunately she could insert Sandling's name into that particular scenario and it would ring just as true.

Klein took one step toward her, halving the already meager distance between them. "I guess I wasn't clear enough when I phoned you. I told you I wouldn't be pulled back into this, and I meant it."

Jason put his hand on the butt on his Glock. "Since we're clearing things up, you won't be calling Lilly again. And you won't be getting in her face to issue any other threats."

No more steps toward her, but that didn't stop Klein's expression from tightening. "She and her father ruined my life."

"And you had no part in that?" Lilly asked.

"None," Klein quickly answered.

Jason obviously didn't buy a word of it. Glaring, he motioned toward the room behind them. "Escort him into interrogation," Jason told O'Reilly. He waited until O'Reilly had done that before he continued. "I need to be here during the questioning, but I'll get someone to give you a ride back to the house."

Yet another head-against-a-brick-wall moment. "And if I don't want to go?" she asked.

"Tough. You're going." He leaned in closer, until his mouth was practically right against her ear. "You've had a long day, an even longer night, and you need some rest. Please, just go. You don't have to worry about being there alone with Erica. I'll make sure an officer stays there with you until I get back."

She was about to argue, but O'Reilly came out of the interrogation room where he'd deposited Klein.

"Before you listen to Klein being grilled, you might want to hear what the crime lab had to say about that surveillance video taken from the security camera at the gate of your neighborhood." O'Reilly closed the door to the interrogation room. "They were able to partially enhance the image," he explained.

Lilly couldn't help it. Her hopes soared. This could be the break they'd been praying for.

"And were they able to determine who was behind the wheel of that car?" Jason asked.

"No."

She'd had mere seconds of that soaring hope, but that dashed them.

"But they were able to get a better look at the license plate," O'Reilly continued. "They only got a partial, but it was enough to run it through DMV and come up with a name."

All right. That was a reason to hope again. "Which is it—Wayne Sandling or Raymond Klein?" Lilly asked.

O'Reilly shook his head. "Neither. The car is registered to your former secretary, Corinne Davies."

Chapter Nine

Jason unlocked the front door to his house,
stepped inside and listened for any sound
that shouldn't have been there. He could hear
the hum of the air-conditioner. The rhythmic
swish of the brass pendulum in the grandfa-
ther clock in the foyer. The TV was on low
volume in the living room.

All seemed well, but he wasn't about to
take that at face value.

Yes, he was paranoid.

That could happen when only ten hours
earlier someone had come close to killing
Lilly and him.

There was a plainclothes cop watching TV
from the sofa in the living room. Jason nodded
and tried to convey his appreciation that the
man was guarding the place in his absence.
Unfortunately, the guards were a necessary

precaution that might have to continue for a while.

Jason didn't even want to think about how long a *while* might be.

He continued down the hall. Listening. Staying vigilant. Erica was in the playroom, and even though she was holding a magazine, Jason didn't think she was reading it. She tossed it aside and practically leaped to her feet when she saw him. But Jason motioned for her to sit back down.

"Where's Megan and Lilly?" he whispered.

There was little change in Erica's expression, just a soft intake of breath that had a hint of frustration to it, and she aimed her index finger in the direction of Lilly's room. "Lilly insisted on having Megan with her," she said.

Uh-oh.

That had probably caused an argument or two. Not from Megan. But from Erica. Things had probably not gone smoothly while he'd been at headquarters. Still, it couldn't be helped. He'd had to do reports and he'd wanted to help with the investigation and interrogation of the suspects. Plus, Lilly had needed some rest. And it was a necessity to get her out of headquarters, away from Wayne Sandling and Raymond Klein. For that to happen, he'd had no choice but to send her with the police escort back to the house. Unfortunately, that meant Lilly had had to deal with Erica on her own. He was sorry he hadn't been here to run interference.

Jason turned toward Lilly's room, and because the door was open, he spotted her immediately. She was napping not on her bed but on a brightly colored patchwork quilt stretched out on the carpeted floor.

She had a sleeping Megan cradled in her arms.

He smiled, leaned his shoulder against the door frame and watched them. This was one of his favorite moments—watching Megan sleep. When she was awake, she was always on the move, and it was impossible to concentrate on the sheer joy she'd brought to his life. But now, with her resting peacefully, Jason could study her tiny face and relive all the wonderful things that he loved about her. If he accomplished every career goal he would ever have, it wouldn't come close to the fulfillment he'd gotten just by being Megan's dad.

And that brought him back to Lilly.

She could take fatherhood from him, but he no longer thought that she would. He mentally shrugged. Maybe that was what he wanted to believe, anyway.

The files that Lilly had brought from her office were scattered on the desk tucked in the corner. She'd no doubt been reading through them while watching Megan. Double duty. He'd done a lot of that himself over the past eleven and a half months.

"Lilly's rushing things," Erica whispered, walking up behind him. She folded her arms over her chest and didn't take her gaze from Lilly. "It'll confuse Megan."

Jason made a sound to indicate he didn't agree. "Megan doesn't look confused or rushed." She looked as if she belonged right there in Lilly's arms.

Erica stayed quiet a few moments, and Jason braced himself for the fallout. It came. "I don't know how you can welcome her into your home. Not after what she did to Greg."

Fallout, indeed. Any other time, he might have agreed. But this wasn't any other time. It was *now,* and whether he wanted it or not, things were changing between Lilly and him. They had to change, for Megan's sake.

"Oh, I get it," Erica concluded on a rise of breath. "You're being nice to Lilly because you're worried she'll take Megan. That's it, isn't it?"

He wished that was it. Jason wished the attraction he felt for Lilly was all part of the custody issue and the love both of them felt for Megan.

But it wasn't.

He wanted to kiss Lilly. He wanted her in his bed. Hell, he just plain wanted her. That didn't have a thing to do with Megan.

"Please don't tell me you're willing to have a relationship with Lilly for Megan's sake?" Erica went on.

Jason didn't know the answer, and he didn't want to explore it now. Especially not with Erica.

Because this wasn't going to be pleasant, he gently took Erica by the arm and led her down the hall so they wouldn't wake Megan and Lilly. He only hoped there wouldn't be shouting, but it was a distinct possibility.

He considered several ways to go about

this, but decided to use the direct approach. "Erica, I think it's time for you to leave."

She went board-stiff. Stared at him. And then jerked away from him as if he'd slapped her. "What do you mean?"

He continued with the direct approach. "I mean that Lilly and I have enough to deal with right now, and your being here isn't making things easier."

"I see." Keeping her gaze pinned to him, she stepped back. She swallowed hard. "Did Lilly talk you into doing this?"

"You know I can't be talked into anything that I don't feel is right. This was my idea. Lilly needs time to be with Megan, and Megan needs time to be with her. That won't happen with you around. Megan will keep turning to you, and that'll only cause friction between Lilly and you."

Erica pulled in a breath and gave a shaky nod. "You're certain about this?"

"Positive. I'll give you a month's severance pay and a reference, but I want you to consider this your two weeks' notice—"

"Two weeks' notice isn't necessary. I'll leave today—for Megan's sake. And yours." Erica looked down at the floor. "I'll pack a few things and arrange for someone to pick up the rest. I won't be long."

"There's no need for you to rush."

"Yes. There is." When she lifted her head again, Jason had no trouble seeing the tears in her eyes.

Great. He felt like a jerk. But he would have felt like a bigger jerk if Lilly had had to battle Erica just so she could spend time with her daughter. This was definitely a case of one too many moms.

Swiftly wiping away her tears, Erica headed in the direction of her room, but then stopped and turned back around to face him. "I'm sorry things didn't work out so I could stay. And just for the record, no hard feelings." With that, she walked away.

Jason was a little surprised with her reaction. It was amicable and the decent thing to say. The *right* thing. If Erica was sincere, that is. But he wondered if she truly was.

"Anything wrong?" He looked back to see Lilly standing in the doorway of her room.

Man, she was a welcome sight, and there was no amount of denial that would make him feel otherwise. There went another slam of guilt. First, over Erica. Now, over this giddy feeling he got whenever he saw Lilly. It'd been that way since he'd kissed her the night before at her office.

Since giddy and guilt just didn't go together with a police investigation, Jason renewed his vow to start rebuilding some barriers between Lilly and him. Not anger barriers. Not hate. Just a few mental fences to remind him that this was a woman his brother had loved. Even if he wanted her—and, yep, he did—having her would make them both miserable.

He needed to remember that.

She'd changed since he'd last seen her at headquarters and now wore a sleeveless silk dress that was the color of ripe peaches. One of the articles of clothing she'd no doubt had the cops pick up for her from her house. The dress suited her, skimming along her body and stopping several inches above her knees so that it exposed a great deal of her legs.

She was barefoot, and he could see that she'd painted her toenails pearl white. For some reason, even with the guilt-producing discussion he'd just had with Erica and the guilt/giddy pep talk he'd given himself, those bare feet captured his attention.

"What happened?" She followed his

gaze to her feet and flexed her eyebrows. "Am I about to get a lecture on the dangers of going barefoot?"

"Not from me." He forced a smile because he thought they could both use it.

"So, what's wrong?"

"Erica's leaving." He kept his voice low so he wouldn't wake Megan. Erica would want to say goodbye to her, of course, but he hoped she would save that goodbye for another day. "She's packing her things now. Once she's done, I'll have the officer drive her where she wants to go."

Lilly's eyes widened, and she walked closer, until they were only a few inches apart. She touched his arm and it soothed him far more than it should have.

"I'm sorry," she whispered.

"Don't be. It's for the best." He hoped. Jason also hoped that Erica's cool farewell wasn't a smoke screen for some sinister plan.

Yep.

That paranoia was still hanging around and was snowballing out of control. It was mixing with Lilly's scent and creating a fog in his brain. She smelled like cinnamon applesauce. Not exactly a scent that would normally turn him on, but it seemed to be doing the trick today.

"How's Megan?" he asked. Best to keep the conversation on a safe topic.

She gave him a suspicious look, as if she'd expected him to say something else. But what he had on his mind, he had no intentions of saying.

"Megan's napping." Lilly checked her watch. "She fell asleep about fifteen minutes ago."

So, it'd be at least an hour, probably twice that long, before she woke up. That would give Erica plenty of time to pack and it'd give him plenty of time to fill Lilly in on what had happened.

"Did you find out anything about Corinne's car?" Lilly worked her fingers through the crown of her hair to scoop it away from her face.

"Yes." And Jason hadn't cared for the news any more than Lilly probably would. "Corinne reported it stolen, but she didn't do that until several hours after the incident at the security gate."

Lilly bunched up her forehead. "Why'd she take so long to report it?"

He'd asked himself the same thing. "Corinne said she didn't notice that her vehicle was missing until she left work that evening. It wasn't in the parking lot so she claims she has no idea who took it or when."

"Do you believe her?"

Jason shrugged. "I don't know what to believe. And it gets even better—guess who works in the same building as Corinne? Raymond Klein and Wayne Sandling. They're partners in the consulting business these days, and they work just three offices away from her."

"Sandling and Klein," Lilly repeated. She pulled in a hard breath. "Their names keep coming up."

Yeah, and not in a good way, either. Either of them was brassy enough to have taken Corinne's car and driven it to the security gate.

"So, we're not taking Corinne off our list of suspects?" Lilly asked.

"No one's coming off that list just yet," he mumbled, rubbing his hand over his face. "Worse, I might have to add a name to it."

Lilly didn't have to think about that for very long. "Erica?"

Jason didn't know why it surprised him that Lilly had come up with the correct answer so quickly. After all, they'd had that whole trust discussion at headquarters. Plus, Lilly had spent the better part of a week under the same roof with Megan's soon-to-be-former nanny. Lilly probably hadn't missed the jealousy in Erica's eyes. He certainly hadn't. Just as he hadn't missed Erica's cool pseudo-goodbye that he feared would come back to haunt them.

Was Erica bitter enough to do something to get rid of Lilly?

Maybe even bitter enough to want to kill her?

"The day that Corinne's car was at the security gate, Erica was here inside with us and couldn't have done it," Lilly pointed out.

Jason had already considered and dismissed that. "It doesn't mean she's innocent, though. She could have hired someone to do the job."

"You mean a hit man?" Lilly shook her head. "No way. She wouldn't have risked that, not with Megan in the house. I might not be on her list of favorite people, but she loves Megan, and she wouldn't have put her in harm's way."

He couldn't dispute that. But there was another angle to this. "Maybe the person in that car was never meant to come inside and hurt you. Maybe it was simply a scare tactic to send you running so that Erica could have Megan all to herself."

"I'm sorry you believe that," he heard Erica say.

Oh, sheez. Open mouth, insert size-twelve boots. And here he hadn't thought this could get any harder.

Erica was at the end of the hall, her suitcase in her hand, and she had a fierce grip on the handle. She didn't come any closer, but her eyes darkened when she looked at Lilly. "You might have won this round, but this isn't over."

"This *round?*" Lilly repeated. "This isn't a competition, Erica."

"Isn't it? You think because you share DNA with Megan that it'll make you her mother? It won't."

"DNA is just for starters," Jason countered. He maneuvered himself in front of Lilly in case Erica decided to go berserk. "The rest will come with time. Lilly has a right to be with her daughter."

He hadn't choked on the words, either. And he wasn't especially shocked that he'd meant every word.

Erica stared at him. "Does she?"

Well, it wasn't the pseudo-cool goodbye that she'd issued just minutes earlier. "I'm ready to go now," Erica said to the officer in the living room. She didn't wait for him. She practically stormed toward the front door.

The detective followed Erica, and from over his shoulder, he issued Jason a nod. Probably of sympathy. Man, he'd really gone about this the wrong way. Of course, maybe there was no correct way to dissolve a relationship like the one that Erica had with Megan.

Erica didn't look back at him when she left, and Jason stood there and watched as the officer shut the door behind them.

"I'm sorry," Lilly repeated.

"So am I, but this had to be done. It's bad enough having suspects out there in the city. I couldn't have one under the same roof."

"Still, that didn't make it easier."

No. It didn't. But he thought his decision might allow him to sleep a little easier tonight.

"There's another problem with Erica being a suspect," Lilly continued. She went to the door, locked it and reactivated the security system. "Wasn't she here at the house with Megan the night someone tried to smother me?"

Since he'd already mentally gone over this info, he knew the answer to that one. "Erica had the night off, and my neighbor was here to watch Megan."

"Oh." She leaned her back against the door. "Okay, so that really could mean that Erica's a suspect."

It did. And it completely changed the motive for what was happening. Of course, that didn't mean Erica was the sole culprit. Jason simply couldn't picture Erica perched on a rooftop shooting at them with a high-powered rifle. So, did that mean there was more than one person after Lilly? Was this some conspiracy, or was it simply two people with two totally different sinister agendas?

"You look exhausted," Lilly observed.

Maybe because he was. Past exhaustion, really. He kept that to himself and switched to a more comfortable topic. "What did Megan and you do all morning?"

Her mouth curved slightly. A brief, amused smile. And she took a step toward him. Slowly. Not some calculated saunter, either. The limp threw off any chance of a seductive stance, and yet that limp, that slight imperfection, made her look all the more human.

As if he needed anything to do that.

"Hmm. Is that question a ploy to distract me from telling you that you look exhausted, or do you really want to know?" Lilly asked.

Well, it was clear that Lilly wasn't going to allow this to be a safe conversation. "Both."

No amused smile that time. Instead, Lilly cleared her throat. "When did we start being so…honest with each other?"

Jason went to her. So they could keep their conversation soft and not wake Megan. Or at least, that's the reason he gave himself for closing the already narrow distance between them. However, to stop himself from doing anything too stupid, he crammed his hands into his jeans' pockets and promised himself that that's where he'd keep them.

"You think we're being honest?" he asked.

Caution flickered in her eyes. They were more blue today than green, and shimmered.

"Probably not. It's hard to have a momentous air-clearing that could lead to total honesty meltdown while people keep trying to kill us." She paused. Frowned. "And there is an *us* in danger now. Thanks to me. Just call me Typhoid Lilly."

"So you're blaming yourself for some homicidal maniac shooting at us?" Jason asked.

"The gunman was aiming for me, and that's what put you in danger." Groaning and burying her face in her hands, she slid down and sat on the floor with her back against the front door. "I keep going over what happened. I keep kicking myself. Conditioned response—indeed. Go to my office to try to trigger some memories. And what happens? I nearly get you killed in the process."

Jason waited a moment. "Are you finished beating yourself up?" He went closer, eased his hands from his pockets and stooped down so they were at eye level.

Lilly met him at that eye level when she lowered her hands from her face. And she ignored his question. "It wasn't enough for me to be negligent in Greg's death, but last night, I almost did the same to you."

Jason didn't like the sound of that. He waited another moment. "*Now* are you finished?"

"No. I'm just getting started."

That pained look on her face intensified. It made him want to comfort her. But pulling her into his arms would mean touching her. And he knew for a fact that just wasn't a good idea. Not with the fatigue and this dangerous energy between them.

Still, he couldn't make himself turn away.

He couldn't stop himself from listening.

And he couldn't stop the ache he had for her.

Because this was forbidden. Taboo. And for some reason that only made him want her more.

"I replay the moments leading up to the shooting," Lilly continued, obviously not willing to drop the subject. "I replay the moments before Greg walked out of my house. I keep thinking if I could just go back and change things—"

"You can't."

Lilly blinked and seemingly listened for answers he couldn't give her. "But then how do I get past it, huh? How do you ever get to the point where you can forgive me? Where I can forgive myself?"

It was a question he'd asked himself at least a thousand times. "I don't know," he said honestly. "But I know blaming yourself won't do any good."

"Maybe not any good, but I don't see how we can avoid it." She raked her finger over her eyebrow. "And how do we get past this... stuff we're feeling for each other?"

"That's a fantastic question," he mumbled.

"Do you have a fantastic answer?"

He shook his head and met her gaze. Not good. It only made him want to move closer to her, and he was already too close as it was. "Lilly, I don't even have a bad answer. Truth is...I don't have any kind of answer at all."

"But you agree that feeling this way is wrong, that it'll only make things more complicated?"

"I agree. Massive complications. And there's that part about it causing us to lose focus while there's all this danger around us."

"Good point," she conceded. She didn't exactly sound thankful for his reminding her of that, either. Which was a good thing.

Because Jason hoped the reminder would make her move away.

It sure as heck wasn't working for him.

But she didn't move. Lilly sat there, her attention fastened to him. She gave him no sultry come-on looks. No whispered invitations. No anything. Still, it happened. The air stirred between them. Everything stirred.

Especially his body.

Jason might have talked himself out of what he was thinking about doing. *Might.* But he didn't even try. Somewhere along the way, he'd lost the battle with reason and was functioning on some primitive level where desire replaced common sense.

Cursing himself, cursing her, cursing this unquenchable need he had for her, Jason leaned forward, slid his hand around the back of her head and tugged her closer to him.

The fire was instant. No more smoldering flames. This was white-hot, and it burned through him. Consuming him. He couldn't think. Couldn't talk. But he could feel. And right now, that was the only thing he wanted to do.

He wanted to feel Lilly in his arms.

Feel his mouth on her.

He wanted to feel everything.

Jason took her as if he owned her. Her lips, pressing against his. Her body, moving against his. Soon, it wasn't enough. Not nearly enough. He tested the taste of her, touching his tongue to hers, and he quickly realized that her taste only made him want her more.

The battle started. The frenzied need for them to touch each other. They fought, grappling for position until Lilly maneuvered her way into his lap.

The kiss continued.

They took and ravished. And took some more. Both starving for what the other was so willing to give.

Jason finally broke the intimate contact when he remembered that he needed air to live. Lilly gulped in some much-needed breaths, as well, while she clung to him.

"What about Megan?" she asked, her voice broken by her breathing.

He'd already thought of that. "We'll hear her if she wakes up," Jason promised.

Lilly nodded, obviously not ready to question that, and she latched on to him and went back for more.

The second battle was just as intense. No longer content with just her mouth, Jason took his kisses to her neck. Lilly made a sound. A low, sensual moan. Definitely not a request for him to stop.

So, Jason didn't stop.

Chapter Ten

Somewhere in the back of her mind, Lilly realized this was a massive mistake.

She knew all the arguments and knew them well. Jason was Greg's brother. The man who could challenge her for custody. The man who had in the past and could continue to make her life a living Hades.

But she no longer cared about arguments and such.

She took things from Jason that she hadn't even known she wanted. The strength from his embrace. The mind-blowing thrill of his kisses. And, mercy, he was a good kisser. The gentleness of his touch. The need. Most of all, the need. She could feel it all through him, and it only fed her own desire for him.

Lilly decided to take everything he was

giving her since there was no chance she'd talk her body, or his, into slowing down. There was a frantic urgency in their kisses. It was a race, but against what she didn't know. All that mattered was that they had to have each other now.

He took her neck. She took his. And she touched. Really touched. Letting her palm slide down all those toned, firm pecs. And his rock-hard abs. She was guessing that he had a six-pack, and she shoved up his shirt to confirm that.

Yes, the man was built.

Jason touched, too. And he was decidedly better at it than she was. While he cupped her neck with one hand and kissed her blind, he let that other clever hand wander in the direction of her right breast. Somehow, even through the fabric of her silk dress and her bra, he managed to locate her nipple, and he pinched it lightly. Just enough pressure to make her want him to do it again and again and again.

"Yes." She let him know in case he'd missed the needy sounds she was making.

"Yes?" Jason questioned, meeting her gaze. But he obviously already knew the answer because he gave her another of those little pinches.

"Yes," she assured him.

Maybe because they now had eye contact, it occurred to her that she should suggest that they stop. But her body promptly disagreed with that. She was hot and aching for him to do more than merely pinch. Mercy, she wanted him.

He pulled her back to him and buried his face in her hair. His breath hit against her neck. It was warm. Quick. His pulse and heartbeat must have been pounding because she could feel it wherever they touched. And they seemed to be touching everywhere.

Except in the very place she wanted him to touch most.

Jason obviously guessed what she wanted because he looped his arm around her waist and pulled her against him. Lilly made adjustments. No easy feat with her legs still not functioning a hundred percent, but she somehow managed to put her knees on each side of his hips.

She moved forward. Saw stars. Really big stars. Then the vee of her panties struck right against the front of his jeans. Lilly could feel him. Every inch of him. That hard ridge straining against the denim.

His mouth was on her neck. Pressing. He slid his hand up her thigh to the front of her panties. Since she'd already moved past into the shameless zone, because every part of her was on fire, Lilly moved against his fingers. Intimately. But not gently. She didn't want gentle. She wanted to feel alive. She wanted to feel needed. She wanted to—

He hooked his fingers onto the elastic of her panties.

And he slipped his hand inside.

Every coherent or semicoherent thought she had flew right out of her head.

"Touch me," she heard herself whisper.

Jason cooperated. He touched her, and he didn't have any trouble finding the right place. Nor was he especially gentle. He made rough, almost frantic slippery strokes. While his mouth feasted on her cheek and neck. While his erection pressed against her thigh. Until she couldn't think. Until she couldn't breathe. Until she didn't care if she ever did either of those things again.

But even without the ability to think or breath, Lilly knew it was time to take this to the next level. She reached for his zipper. Jason took it up a notch, as well. He shoved her dress up to her waist.

Then he stopped.

And stared at her.

Lilly blinked, trying to focus. Trying to figure out what had happened to bring everything to an abrupt halt.

"I don't have a condom."

Oh, great. Somehow, even through her passion-hazed brain, she understood that. She also understood she didn't have an immediate solution. "Neither do I."

He cursed. It was a four-letter word for what they would be doing if they'd had a condom.

"I don't guess there's one in the house somewhere?" she asked. And she was hoping the answer was yes.

Jason shook his head. "I haven't had a woman here."

Because of Megan. Lilly understood that. Her body didn't like it, but she understood it.

Logic and normalcy slowly began to return, little by little, and with each passing second, she began to feel more and more self-conscious. The passion began to fade.

So did the immediate, pressing need to have wild sex on the floor with Jason.

All right, she couldn't lie to herself. She still had that particular need for wild sex, but it was stupid to have pushed things this far without at least making a few rudimentary plans—like buying a condom.

Frustrated, she eased out of his lap and pulled her dress back into place so that she was covered. She hadn't minded her seminudity during the crazy foreplay, but it seemed awkward now.

"Please don't say you're sorry that happened," he whispered.

She dodged his gaze. "Sorry isn't the correct word. Embarrassed."

"Why? Because we acted on what we've been feeling for days?"

Lilly debated several answers but went with the truth. "This whole lack-of-condom thing reminds me a little of teenagers with their hormones out of control. Plus, I'm not sure sex would have been a smart idea."

"It wouldn't have been smart," Jason readily concurred. He paused, smiled. Dimples flashed. "But it would have been damn good."

She couldn't help it. She laughed. Lilly savored the light moment, but at the same time she knew it did nothing to cut the tension that was so thick she could taste it.

"Once we find out who's trying to kill us," he said, sounding as disappointed and as unfulfilled as Lilly felt, "we can concentrate on what's happening, or not happening, between us."

Yes, that was logical.

Maybe a little too logical, considering that he was still aroused. And that got Lilly thinking.

What *had* just happened?

She thought about keeping the question to herself. Maybe mulling it over for a while. But Jason was here, right in front of her, and before the kissing and touching, they'd had this whole honesty discussion going on between them.

"I have to know. All this kissing and touching—does it have anything to do with Megan?" Lilly asked.

That seemed to freeze him for several seconds. "Excuse me?"

After seeing his reaction, she instantly regretted her question. But there was no turning back now. Even if it hurt like the devil, she had to know the truth. "Is this your way of working out a custody arrangement?"

No freezing that time. Her question earned her a scalpel-sharp glare, and he had to unclench his teeth before he could speak. "I'm going to pretend I didn't hear that."

She caught his arm to stop him when he started to get up. "No, you're not. You're going to search your heart and tell me if that's what you're really feeling."

And judging from the arctic look on Jason's face, she wouldn't like his answer. JASON WANTED NOTHING more than to dismiss Lilly's question, but he couldn't.

Hell.

One minute, they were all wrapped up in each other's arms, sharing hot kisses and on the verge of having equally hot sex. Now, he felt as if he were facing a firing squad.

And facing a moment of truth.

Lilly had simply asked what had been on his mind for days, and it was time to deal with it.

"If a relationship of convenience is what it takes for us both to be with Megan, will you consider it?" he asked, hoping she didn't slap him.

But if she had intentions of slapping him, Lilly didn't follow through on them. That's because they heard the sound at the end of the hall. Little footsteps. A moment later, the owner of those little footsteps appeared, and Megan toddled toward them.

Lilly did a double check to make sure they were both decent. They were. And she smiled at Megan. The little girl returned the smile. A sleepy one. She had woken up a little too early from her nap.

Megan stopped when she was just a few inches away and gave each of them a considering look. Obviously she felt she had some sort of decision to make. It didn't take her long, though. She went to Jason, sank down next to him and rested her head against his arm.

It was one of those magic moments that he'd been lucky enough to share often with Megan. He treasured times like this. However, he knew these were no longer just Megan's and his moments. He picked up Megan, kissed her cheek and deposited her onto Lilly's lap.

Jason didn't know which of them was most surprised by that.

Megan look confused. Lilly, stunned. And he was sure he was both. Still, Megan didn't protest the new arrangement. She settled against Lilly and closed her eyes to finish her nap.

Lilly lifted her eyes to meet his. *Thank you,* she mouthed.

He braced himself for some feelings of jealousy, but those feelings thankfully didn't come. Progress, indeed.

"Well?" he prompted. "Would you consider a relationship of convenience?"

Lilly moistened her lips and looked down at Megan. "I'd consider almost anything for her sake. But we're already facing an obstacle or two in the convenience department. Sometimes the fire and heat burn out and leave a lot of bitterness. When that happens, it doesn't make anything convenient."

Jason didn't have to ask her to clarify. He knew. And unfortunately, he also knew she was probably right. But was there enough common ground between them to overcome anything? He didn't get a chance to pose that question to her because the phone in the living room rang. Since it could have something to do with security or the investigation, Jason quickly got up to answer it.

"Detective Lawrence, it's me, Corinne Davies," the caller said. "We met the other night at Lilly's office."

"I know who you are," he informed her. After the incident with the stolen car, both her name and voice were imprinted on his brain. What he couldn't figure out was what the heck she was doing calling him. "How can I help you?"

She didn't answer right away. "I hope I haven't made a mistake by contacting you, but I think I might have found some information you need."

That got his full attention. "I'm listening." And so that Lilly could do the same, he turned on the speaker function of the phone.

"I was going through some old files I had from when I worked for Lilly. I found some e-memos that Raymond Klein sent to Lilly's father." Her words were suddenly rushed, as if she was trying to hurry. "They seem to suggest that they were about to do something illegal. Something to do with paying off a city official so they could undercut other bids for a building project. One of those other bids appears to belong to your brother, Greg."

Jason met Lilly's gaze. She didn't appear surprised, but concerned. She pulled Megan protectively closer to her.

"I'll want to see these memos," Jason told Corinne.

"I thought you would. But there might be a problem. The files might have been tampered with." Corinne's voice dropped even lower. She was either very nervous and frightened about this call, or else she was putting on a good act. "I can't verify that this e-memo even came from Klein. I'm usually pretty good at unraveling the e-mail addresses and identities of the senders, but this one has been blocked. I can't be sure if this information in the memo is correct or if someone planted it to make it look as if something illegal was going on."

After hearing that, Jason had a dilemma of his own. Was Corinne up to something? He certainly didn't trust the woman, and that lack of trust cast some serious suspicion on what she was saying. However, he couldn't just dismiss potential evidence either, especially if that evidence could be used to convict Raymond Klein.

"Take what you have to police headquarters," Jason instructed Corinne. "I'll pick it up there."

"I can't do that."

"And why not?"

More hesitation. Jason could practically see the woman wringing her hands, or else pretending to wring them. "I think someone's watching me. Maybe it has something to do with what happened to Lilly. The shooting, I mean. I don't want to go walking into police headquarters because I believe someone will try to stop me from doing that."

Well, he could understand her concern. Jason could also understand his own concern. "You can fax or copy the files and e-mail them," he suggested.

"No, I can't. Some are handwritten, and the ink is very pale. I tried to copy a few, but they're barely even legible in places."

Oh, man. He didn't even want to know where this was leading.

"I want to meet with Lilly and you so I can give you the files in person," Corinne insisted.

Lilly made a frustrated sound and shook her head.

Jason agreed. "It wouldn't be safe for Lilly to be out in public."

"I can meet you someplace safe," Corinne insisted.

But Jason knew there were no real safe places. Especially not for a meeting with a suspect.

"You choose the location," Corinne continued. She no longer sounded just afraid. She sounded desperate. "You bring along extra cops. Guns, whatever. Do what you need to do to secure the place, and I'll give you what I found."

Jason quickly thought that through and came up with a solution. "All right. Let's meet in the parking lot of police headquarters, but Lilly won't be coming with me."

"She has to, or else I'll call the whole thing off. I don't really know you, Detective Lawrence, but I know Lilly, and I know she wouldn't do anything to hurt me. That's why I insist that she be there."

"Okay," he heard Lilly say.

Glaring at her hardly seemed enough to convey his displeasure for her okay. "Lilly won't be coming with me," Jason insisted.

"I'll be at the parking lot of the downtown

police headquarters at 8:00 p.m.," Corinne said. "If Lilly's not there, I won't be, either."

And with that ultimatum, she hung up.

"We have to meet her. You know we don't have a choice about this," Lilly said immediately.

"Oh, but we do, and that choice is for you to stay put. I'll go to the meeting and get those memos and files from Corinne while you stay here under police guard."

Lilly's frown probably meant she didn't agree with his plan. "What if she means what she said? What if she won't meet with you if I'm not there?"

Jason considered that, and dismissed it. "What if she's up to something?"

"What if she's not?" Lilly argued.

He huffed. "How long are you going to keep countering a question with a question?"

She made a show of pretending to think about it. "Forever?"

That didn't improve his mood. "Smart-ass."

"So I've been told. But here's the deal, Jason. Corinne wants to meet in the parking lot of police headquarters. If she had murder on her mind, she wouldn't have chosen a place where she'd likely get arrested. Pardon the question, but would she?"

Maybe. Or maybe this was one smart ploy to get them to cooperate.

And a ploy to get them killed.

"I don't like this," Jason told her.

"Neither do I. That's why I'll stay in the car. In fact, we both will, and we'll let Corinne come to us."

Jason stared at her. And glared. He hoped it conveyed his displeasure. But what it probably also conveyed was that Lilly had a point. Corinne might have something they needed.

"You won't meet face-to-face with Corinne even if she insists?" Jason asked.

"I might have a smart mouth, but I'm not stupid." Lilly brushed a kiss on Megan's forehead. "Besides, I have a very important reason for staying alive, and I'm holding that reason right here in my arms."

Jason looked down at Megan. Before he ever switched on the speakerphone, he'd known that she'd fallen asleep. Megan seemed totally unaware of what was happening. Thank goodness. That was something at least. The stress and worry of their situation hadn't spilled over to her.

"Those memos that Corinne found could be the very thing we need to put an end to all of this," Lilly pointed out.

And she was right. Jason knew it. So did she.

That didn't make this easier, though.

"I'll get another officer to stay here with Megan," Jason finally said. "I'll also arrange for us to use an unmarked vehicle with bulletproof windows. You and I will drive to headquarters, but you won't be getting out of the car. Right?"

"Right," she promised.

That promise might keep her safe. *Might.* But Jason couldn't help but wonder if he was about to lead Lilly straight into a deadly trap.

Chapter Eleven

"I'm kicking myself," Jason mumbled. Though his voice carried almost no sound, Lilly heard him loud and clear. She also felt the knotted muscles in his arm as they sat side by side on the seat of the unmarked car. "You know that, right?"

Lilly knew.

She was kicking herself, as well.

This meeting with Corinne could be important, critical even, but she hated leaving Megan for any reason. It didn't matter that her daughter was in safe hands with not just one cop, but two. It also didn't matter that one of the cops, Sgt. Garrett O'Malley, was someone that she knew and trusted.

Nope.

This didn't have to do with trust. It had to do with leaving her little girl while she tried to figure out who wanted Jason and her dead. High stakes. But with an equally high possibility of failure.

She glanced around the parking lot again and checked her watch. "No sign of Corinne," she pointed out.

Lilly didn't have to add that the woman was nearly a half hour late. Jason was well aware of that. He was probably also well aware that Corinne wasn't going to show with the evidence and this had perhaps been some sort of wild-goose chase.

But why would Corinne have done that?

Lilly couldn't come up with a good answer, but there were possibilities that made her uncomfortable. In addition to the wild-goose theory, maybe someone had blackmailed Corinne into arranging this meeting. And that led Lilly right back to Wayne Sandling and Raymond Klein.

"She's not going to show," Jason declared.

Even though it was dark, there were enough security lights in the parking lot for her to note his frustrated, impatient expression. Sighing and feeling equally impatient and frustrated, she leaned her head against the glass of the heavily tinted window.

"Maybe the officers you sent out to check the area will find her," Lilly answered. "Maybe she's out there, waiting to make sure it's safe before she comes into the open."

"Maybe," he said, not sounding as if he believed that. She didn't believe it, either. "Don't sit so close to the window."

She glanced at the window. Frowned. "I thought they were bulletproof."

"More like bullet resistant. If the shooter is using armor-piercing bullets, the shot could still get through."

He didn't have to say that twice. Lilly immediately slid across the seat toward him, until her arm was squashed against his again. He felt warm. Comforting. Something she desperately needed.

"There are too many things that could go wrong," Jason said under his breath. "That's obviously why I didn't want you to come."

"But if something goes right, and we get these memos from Corinne, you might have the evidence you need for an arrest. Then we won't be in danger anymore."

He stayed quiet a moment. "If this doesn't work, maybe you could try going about this from a different angle. During some investigations when the witness has been traumatized, sometimes we use a psychiatrist to hypnotize the person, to see if they recall anything."

Lilly considered that. "And it's been successful?" she asked.

"Sometimes."

"Well, sometimes is better than nothing. I'll do it. Just let me know when and where." In fact, she wished they'd already arranged it. Recalling the face of the person who'd tried to kill her might lead them to the person who was behind all these latest attempts on their lives.

"Let's get past this rendezvous first," Jason reminded her.

If there was a rendezvous. And if it would amount to anything. They could be back at square one, and that meant all of them were in danger.

Including Megan.

Only hours earlier Jason had asked her if she would consider a relationship of convenience. Ironic. Because with the danger staring them right in their faces, she should be considering just the opposite. To keep her child and Jason safe, she might have to consider doing the unthinkable.

She might have to leave.

In some ways that was unimaginable. And yet in other ways, it seemed irresponsible not to do it. If she left, maybe the person trying to kill her wouldn't go anywhere near Megan. It broke her heart just to consider it, but it would break her heart even more to lose her daughter.

The movement caught Lilly's eye, and she looked up to see two uniformed officers cut across the parking lot. They approached the car, and Jason lowered the window a fraction.

"We found something," one of the officers said to Jason.

"Is it Corinne Davies?" Jason asked.

The rookie shook his head and cast an uneasy glance at Lilly before bringing his gaze back to Jason. "Not exactly. But, trust me, you'll want to see this."

THE ROOKIE'S *You'll want to see this* might have been vague, but it was more than enough to get Jason moving. Obviously, his fellow cop had something to say, and he didn't want to say it in front of Lilly. If that was the case, there wasn't much chance of this being good news.

"I want you to wait here with Lilly," Jason ordered the rookie. He glanced at the other uniformed officer. "You'll come with me."

Jason checked his weapon and opened the door. "Don't let her get out of the car, and don't let Corinne Davies or anyone other than me get anywhere near her, understand?"

The rookie nodded.

Lilly didn't agree quite so quickly. "Wait a minute," she said, grabbing Jason's arm to stop him from leaving. "What if I don't want you to go to check on this 'thing you'll want to see'?"

"It's my job to go," Jason countered.

She pointed first at the rookie and then at the other officer. "It's their job, too. Why can't they go?"

"Because I'm a detective and they're not. Besides, this is personal for me. If Corinne is out there, I want to see her face-to-face, to see if I can figure out what's really going on here."

She frowned. "I don't suppose it'd do any good to ask if I can go with you?"

He didn't even have to think about that. "No good whatsoever. You're staying put."

Jason turned to leave, but she latched on

to his arm again. "Don't do anything…stupid, okay?" And with that, she leaned forward and hurriedly brushed a kiss on his cheek.

It definitely wasn't one of those lusty foreplay kisses they'd shared in the foyer of his house. But in some ways, it packed an even greater wallop. Because it was the kind of kiss that people gave each other when they were more than just two people with a child in common.

How much more? Jason asked himself.

But he pushed the question aside. He was about to venture into what could essentially be a kill zone, and he needed a clear head for that. He didn't want the distraction of his feelings for Lilly to cloud his judgment.

"Stay put," he ordered Lilly one last time, and he got out of the car before she could stop him again.

Or before he felt compelled to return that kiss.

"So, did you find Corinne Davies or not?" Jason asked the officer once the door was closed and Lilly could no longer hear what they were saying. If it was bad news, he wanted a chance to process it first before he told her.

"No, but we found a car parked just up the street." They headed in that direction, and Jason looked over his shoulder to cast one last don't-get-out warning glance at Lilly and a watch-her warning glance at the rookie who was now guarding the car.

"The car we found is a rental," the officer continued. "We called the company, and it's Ms. Davies' name on the rental agreement."

Maybe she'd used a rental because she was concerned about being recognized. Or maybe because her other car had been stolen and she hadn't had a chance to replace it. Still, the situation made Jason uneasy. Of course, everything was making him uneasy at this point.

With his hand on his gun, Jason and the officer proceeded out of headquarters' parking lot and onto the sidewalk. He spotted the silver-gray car right away. It was parked in the center point between two streetlights. In others words, in the spot with the least visibility.

There was another uniformed officer waiting by the vehicle. "No sign of Ms. Davies yet," the officer volunteered. "She's not in the car, but we haven't made a thorough search of the area yet."

Jason looked around at the street jammed with buildings on each side. There were plenty of places to hide if Corinne had gone inside one of them. Maybe inside and on the roof with a high-powered rifle? He glanced up, half expecting to see her standing there, with a gun aimed right at him.

But Corinne wasn't anywhere in sight.

Temporarily satisfied that he wasn't about to be ambushed, Jason turned his attention back to the rental car. He borrowed a flashlight from one of the uniformed officers and checked the interior.

Nothing.

No purse, no jacket, no cell. No sign of a struggle.

That didn't mean there hadn't been one.

He put his hand over the hood of the car. He didn't touch the surface in case it became necessary for them to dust for prints. But he could feel no heat coming from the engine. The car had no doubt been parked there for a while. Perhaps even for several hours.

Jason swept the milky light over the exterior of the car, and when he didn't see anything out of the ordinary, he began to examine the street and the sidewalk. It didn't take him long to spot what he'd hoped he wouldn't see.

"Secure the area," Jason ordered the officers. "And get the CSI guys out here now."

Cursing under his breath, Jason angled the flashlight, moving it along the black asphalt. Despite the dark color, he had no trouble seeing the wet spots. Though he already knew what they were, he stooped and touched his index finger to one of the drops.

It was blood.

Chapter Twelve

"Bad news?" Lilly asked. She was lying on the hospital bed, her forearm draped across her forehead.

Jason realized she'd been asking that a lot in the past twenty-four hours. Probably because they hadn't gotten good news about, well, much of anything.

It had been a long day.

And it was going to get a lot longer.

First, there was the hypnosis and then later Lilly was scheduled for one of those marathon physical therapy sessions at the hospital. But it wasn't the hypnosis and the physical therapy that concerned him most. His biggest concern was that it was next to impossible to keep her safe while they were away from the house.

"It must be bad news," she mumbled.

She was right, of course.

Jason pocketed his cell and debated how much he should tell her. After all, she was supposed to be relaxing, waiting for the drug to take effect so she could be hypnotized. She was drowsy, no doubt about that, but since he knew she was anxious for an update, Jason proceeded with the recount that he'd just gotten from a fellow detective.

"Still no sign of Corinne, and the crime scene techs estimate there's about a half a pint of blood on the trail leading away from the car." A trail that stopped one street over. Which meant Corinne had likely gotten into another vehicle. Now the question was, had that happened voluntarily or had she been forced to go? And if it'd been voluntary, why hadn't she gone to the ER? There was one just a few blocks from the scene, yet there was no record of anyone matching her description.

"They're sure it's Corinne's blood?" Lilly asked.

"It's consistent with her blood type. She's not in any of the data banks, so the CSI guys will first need to obtain a sample of her known DNA to compare to what they collected from the scene."

She nodded. Or rather tried to, but it was obvious the drug was taking effect. "She could have faked her injuries."

Jason was surprised she could come up with that theory while under sedation. But he'd already considered it. "You mean, maybe Corinne stockpiled some of her blood and used it to make us think there was foul play?"

Another shaky nod.

It was possible, but if Corinne had done that, it was because she was scared and wanted to make them believe she was no longer alive. Or else she wanted her fake death to allow her the lack of scrutiny from the police so she could finish what she had started. It sent a chill through him to consider what Corinne *might have started.*

"I learned something else," Jason continued. "It's not good news, either. The lab got the results from the clothes that Sandling and Klein were wearing the night of the shooting, and neither showed any signs of gunshot residue."

That proved nothing, of course. There'd been time before their interrogation so they could have changed clothes and given themselves a thorough scrub-down to remove any residue.

The door swung open and Jason automatically reached for his weapon. He stopped, however, when he realized it was the shrink. Dr. Malcolm McCartle. Tall, imposing. A dark tan with a shiny bald head that was less indicative of age than the fashion trend. Thankfully, the doctor had dealt with enough cops and police situations that he didn't even question Jason's actions.

"Lilly, how are you doing?" Dr. McCartle asked. He rolled over a chair, plopped down right next to her bed and took the notepad from the nightstand.

"Fine," she mumbled without even opening her eyes.

The doctor looked up at Jason. "Since she gave permission, you're welcome to stay, but I'd prefer if you didn't ask questions. And don't say anything, for that matter. I have your list of things here that you'd like to know, and I'll go from there."

Jason nodded, took a seat and listened as the doctor murmured words of reassurance to Lilly. It took McCartle several minutes to finish, and then he glanced down at the notepad, where Jason had written the questions. Jason only hoped they were the right questions and that Lilly could answer them.

"Lilly, I want you to think back to the night of your car crash," the doctor instructed, his voice soft and flat. "Nineteen months ago. You leave your office. It's night. The air is chilly because it's winter, and it's drizzling. Do you remember that?"

"Yes. I have on my coat. The black wool one with the silver buttons."

Well, that was a good start. Jason hoped it continued because there were some difficult questions on that list.

"You're walking through the parking lot and you get in your car," Dr. McCartle prompted. "And then you start driving on San Pedro. You head north on Highway 281 to Anderson Loop. Think about that drive, Lilly. Take yourself back to that night. Can you see if anyone is following you?"

Even though her eyes were closed, he could see the movement beneath her lids. "No. I don't think so."

"Look around the inside of your car. Do you have the computer disk with you?"

"Yes," she said quickly. "It's on the front

passenger's seat, next to my purse. It's important. It has a lot of information about my father."

"What kind of information?" the doctor asked.

"Copies of forged and altered agreements and deals. There are some bids and paperwork that he stole so that competing companies wouldn't get city contracts that he wanted. He bribed people. He intimidated them. And I have proof of all of that."

Jason didn't doubt that such proof existed. It was just too bad that the cops hadn't realized just how much danger Lilly was in because she possessed such evidence. If they'd known, they likely could have given her protection and saved her from the accident and the coma.

"Lilly, are you nervous about the disk?" Dr. McCartle questioned.

"Yes." Another fast answer, and her face became tense. "I'm going to take it to the police."

"Does anyone know you're planning to do that?" the doctor asked.

No fast answer that time. Lilly gave it some thought. "I told my secretary, Corinne."

Oh, hell. Now that was a bit of info that Corinne hadn't volunteered. That lent some credence to the theory that Corinne might have faked her own death or injury. Of course, maybe the woman simply forgot to inform them of what she knew. But then, that seemed such an important thing to forget.

"Does anyone else know that you have the disk?" Dr. McCartle read from the list.

"Maybe." Another pause. Her forehead bunched up. "I kept the blinds in my office open all day, well into the evening. Corinne said something about having the feeling that we were being watched, and she was nervous."

Yet another new piece of the puzzle. It didn't exonerate Corinne, but it sure as heck explained how someone else might have known what Lilly was about to do.

"You're in your car now," the doctor continued. "You're driving on Anderson Loop. Traffic is light. You're going through an area where there aren't many businesses. Look around you again. Check the rearview and side mirrors. Is anyone following you?"

Before the doctor spoke the last word of his question, Lilly gasped. Jason bolted to his feet, but without looking at him, the doctor motioned for him to sit down.

"The car's coming right at me," Lilly said, her voice high-pitched and strained. So were the muscles in her face and neck. And she had a death grip on the side of the bed. "My God, it's going to hit me."

Jason couldn't sit. Not listening to that. Not hearing the terror in Lilly's voice.

"Describe the car," McCartle insisted.

She frantically shook her head, and for a moment Jason didn't think she could answer. That this had all been for nothing. But then, the head shaking stopped and her grip relaxed a little. "It's maroon. Dark windows. Four doors. It's coming at me. Fast. So fast. And I'm swerving to get away from it. There's a bridge. God, a bridge!" Lilly's hand flew up to cover her face, and Jason could only imagine how terrified she was. "I slammed into the guardrail."

"It's all right," the doctor assured her. "You won't feel any pain."

"No pain," Lilly repeated several times, as if trying to convince herself. "But I touch my fingers to my forehead, and I see the blood. I'm hurt. I'm dizzy."

Dr. McCartle gently rubbed her arm. "Look around you, Lilly. Do you still see that car that ran you off the road?"

"No. I can't see anything. Everything's spinning around."

The doctor leaned closer to her and lowered his voice to a whisper. "Listen, then. What do you hear?"

She waited a moment, and the movement was almost feverish beneath her eyelids. "Someone's there. Someone's opening the door on my side of the car. But I can't see a face."

"Look carefully," the doctor prompted. "Try to focus."

Jason held his breath. Waiting. And praying this would soon be over so that Lilly wouldn't have to go through any more.

"I can't see the face," Lilly whispered, her voice weak. "It's getting dark. And I can't feel. I don't think I can breathe." She hesitated. "And then everything stops… I stop."

The coma had taken her—and at such a crucial time. A few more minutes, a little better light, and Lilly might have been able to make an ID. Still, Jason wasn't ready to give up.

"Lilly, I want you to go back in time," the

doctor instructed, looking at the notes. "Before the crash. What were you thinking about just before you saw the maroon car?"

It took her a moment to answer. "I was thinking about the disk. About all the problems my father had caused. And I was thinking about Greg."

That got Jason's attention. He motioned for the doctor to continue with that thread of questioning.

"Why Greg?"

"I found some information." Lilly paused, and judging from the way her mouth tightened, she was concentrating hard. "I think maybe Greg had some run-ins with one or more of my father's former business associates."

Well, that confirmed what Corinne had said. And what Jason had suspected.

"I was also thinking about the night Greg and I slept together," Lilly continued. "It was a mistake."

The doctor started to say something, but Lilly spoke before he could.

"I didn't love Greg," she volunteered. "And I told him that. He was angry. Furious. Yelling. He said I didn't love him because I wanted his brother. It was true. I couldn't deny it. I've always been attracted to Jason." She made a dismissal sound deep in her throat. "But I'm not his type."

If he hadn't heard the words come from her mouth, Jason wouldn't have believed them. Whoa. That was a powerful confession. Definitely not the earth-shattering revelation of the identity of a would-be killer, but it was earth-shattering still the same.

So, now he knew. She hadn't been in love with Greg. Instead, she'd been attracted to him.

Him.

Now, the real question was, what was he going to do about it?

LILLY WASN'T HAVING much luck getting Megan to take a nap. Partly because she hated to lose even a couple of hours of time with her daughter—even if a nap was a necessity. On the other hand, judging from Jason's somber mood, he was waiting for Megan to fall asleep so that they could discuss some things. Things she'd no doubt disclosed while under hypnosis.

On the drive back from the hospital, Jason

had said something about Greg being connected to one or more of her father's business associates. Before he could explain, he'd gotten a call. Then another. By the time he'd finished his conversations, they were at the house.

The interruptions hadn't stopped there.

They'd barely made it inside when she heard Megan rather loudly demand a bottle and some attention. Lilly had given Detective Sarah Albright, the "on-duty" nanny, a reprieve and had taken the crying child from her arms. She'd then given Megan a bottle, changed her, had even sung her a lullaby, but her daughter was still whining and obviously exhausted, reacting to all the recent changes in her life and the stress.

As was Jason.

He wasn't rubbing his eyes, but he had that surly, bruised expression. Mercy, she hoped she hadn't talked about sleeping with Greg. Jason shouldn't have been subjected to that.

Lilly pulled herself away from her mental brow-beating and kissed her daughter's cheek. Megan smiled. Not a bright-eyed grin as she often did. It was a lazy kind of smile that was a precursor to her eyelids drifting down. Lilly hummed softly to her, rocked her gently, and Megan finally surrendered to the dreaded nap.

Most would consider getting her daughter to sleep to be a small accomplishment, but for Lilly it was a huge milestone. There'd be many times like this. Milestones of all shapes and sizes, and she intended to be there for all of them.

Lilly struggled when she tried to get out of the chair in the nursery, and she silently cursed her still-weak legs. She was tired of being in recovery when she had so many important and dangerous things happening around her. Heaven forbid if she actually had to outrun a bad guy.

It wouldn't be a pretty sight.

When Jason noticed that she was struggling, he came to the rescue. He gently scooped up the sleeping Megan and eased her into her crib. Lilly gave Megan one last kiss, one last look before she covered her with a blanket, and Jason and she stepped out of the room.

"Okay," Lilly started, "what's wrong?"

He didn't answer her question. "Any leftover effects from the drug the shrink gave you?"

"I'm doing fine." Not exactly the truth. She was exhausted, but she had too many things to do to nap, including the physical therapy appointment that they'd have to leave for within the hour. There'd be time for naps once this rifle-wielding psycho was caught. "I don't think I can say the same for you, though. So, why the glum mood?" Rather than fishing for the answer, she went for the direct approach. "Did I say something about Greg that I shouldn't have?"

He blinked and shook his head. A denial that didn't quite convince her. "You said you thought maybe Greg had had some run-ins with your father's former business associates."

Not exactly news-at-five. Corinne had already said as much.

Jason looked around the hall and made a glance at the living room. "Let's go to my office," he insisted, already leading her in that direction. They passed through the living room where Detective Albright was taking a much-needed break on the sofa.

"I have the files we took from your office

the other day," Jason continued. "And I think I might have found the connection."

Okay. So, maybe there was news, after all, and maybe this was the real reason for his puzzling mood.

Jason's home office was on the other side of the house, next to the kitchen. Lilly had glanced in there a time or two, but she hadn't gone in before now. It was a man's room. Wood floors, ceiling beams, a darkly colored Turkish rug and a desk that dominated the space. She looked around and spotted the baby monitor on the corner of the desk. A little green light indicated it was on, which meant they'd be able to hear Megan if she woke.

"Here," Jason said, pulling up a chair for her. She sat next to him, and he handed her a single sheet of paper. "It's the police's theory that the person who stole the disk from you after the car crash also went through your office and took the files you'd copied. I think the person missed this one. It's a handwritten memo from your father to Wayne Sandling."

She remembered the memo and remembered that she'd copied it onto the disk. It was one of literally hundreds she'd read when she'd been trying to determine the extent of her father's illegal activities. It was basically a vaguely worded "suggestion" for Wayne Sandling to make sure that their latest bid for a municipal contract was accepted. In other words, do whatever necessary to insure no one else outbid them.

"Check the dates," Jason prompted. "And then look at the date of this correspondence from Greg."

Greg's correspondence was a week after her father's memo. Greg had written a letter to the city council, expressing his concern, and fury, over the selection process for a specific contract. A contract he'd lost, even though he'd insisted he'd put in a lower bid than the winning company—a business represented by her father.

Of course.

"There's more," Jason continued. "While you were in recovery from the hypnosis drug, I made some calls. I had one of the detectives read back through Greg's accident report. An eyewitness reported that there was a maroon, four-door car with tinted windows in the vicinity."

Lilly shook her head, not making the connection.

"Under hypnosis, you said the car that hit you was maroon with heavily tinted windows."

She was so glad she was sitting down. No, it wasn't clear-cut evidence, but she couldn't dismiss it as a coincidence, either. "You think Greg might have been murdered?" she asked, holding her breath.

"I think it's a strong possibility."

"Oh, God. Oh, God." She couldn't help it. She dropped her head onto his shoulder and the tears came. The grief was fresh again, as if his death had just happened. "And here all this time, I thought this was my fault. I've been blaming myself."

"And I've been blaming you."

She was aware that along with all the pain they were both no doubt feeling, there were several issues and revelations that had to be dealt with. Greg's death. Jason's and her past.

Maybe even their future.

"What are we going to do about this information?" she muttered, lifting her head from his shoulder.

"*You're* going to do nothing but stay safe. I've already turned all of this over to the lead detective. He's planning a database search to try to identify the car. Of course, it has been nineteen months…"

In other words, it might be too late. The car could be anywhere by now. Still, she had to hold out hope that they'd get lucky.

Since Jason had broached the subject of his brother, Lilly decided to continue it. "While I was under hypnosis, did I say anything else about Greg?"

Jason eased away from her, and he dodged her gaze. "What do you mean?"

Uh-oh. That eluded gaze couldn't be a good sign. Yep, she'd no doubt mentioned sex. Great. Nothing like reminding him of the huge sore spot that was between them. "I just got the feeling that I'd said something to make you uncomfortable."

"No. Not uncomfortable," he insisted. But his hesitation said otherwise. "You just clarified a few things for me."

Another uh-oh. "Like what?"

He shrugged, moved away another inch. "Like how important it is for us to solve this case."

Lilly sighed. She couldn't fault him for his evasive answer. If their positions had been reversed, she wouldn't have wanted to discuss his previous sexual activity. She didn't even want to *think* about it.

"So, we're back to vague responses, chitchat, et cetera?" she mumbled.

"What do you mean?" Jason asked. And he asked it with a straight face, too. Had she misinterpreted his ambiguous response? Or maybe she hadn't said what she thought she'd said while under hypnosis.

"Why won't you tell me what I said that's made you so standoffish?" She heard herself and wanted to wince. Mercy, it was time to drop this. So what if she never learned his—

"I care about you," Jason said, interrupting her thoughts. Thank goodness. Because she truly hadn't wanted to finish that. "But we don't have a clean slate, Lilly. We never will. And I don't know how we deal with that. If—"

"Wait a minute." She slapped her palm on his chest. "Back up to that part about you caring about me."

He looked at her as if her nose were on backward. "Of course I care about you."

"Of course," she repeated. She held up her

left index finger. "Give me a minute for that to sink in."

He shook his head, obviously surprised by her reaction. "I wouldn't have kissed you if I didn't care."

She grunted. "Kissing and caring aren't always related. Sometimes kissing is just about lust and nothing else."

"And sometimes, kissing is about kissing."

Lilly stared at him, trying to figure out what he meant and where this was going. After several long moments, she decided she didn't have a clue.

Did she?

She kept staring at him and unfortunately got a little distracted by his face. His mouth, in particular. And she nearly lost her train of thought. That mouth certainly had her hormonal number.

"So, when we were on the floor by the front door, were we just kissing, lusting…or were we doing something else?" Lilly asked.

He stared at her. Deadpan face. No expression other than maybe slight bewilderment. Then he laughed. Only then did she realize just how suggestive that last part must have sounded.

"I think it falls in the 'something else' category," he said.

Mercy. That sounded suggestive, too. Better yet, his eyes had filled with a warmth that softened the angles of his face. It softened her, too. The man was magic. He could improve her mood with just a look.

"That 'something else' category is a little broad," she stated. "And scary."

Jason nodded, looped his arm around her and pulled her closer. "I'm trying to take things slow. *Slower,*" he amended.

He no longer had that soft, amused look in his eyes. Subtle. But she noticed them, all right. She was aware of everything about him. The edginess that now tightened his mouth. His nostrils flared slightly. He brushed against her.

"Slow can be good, I suppose," she heard herself say. But she had no idea if that was true.

"I suppose," he repeated. More changes. She felt the muscles in his arms tense. The pulse on his throat raced. "Even though I've considered us just having sex to see if it'll burn this energy from us."

Her breath vanished. Just like that. It was

gone. And just like that, she was his for the taking.

"That's an interesting theory." Lilly tried to keep her voice level. And failed. "You think that'll work?"

"No. But my body keeps suggesting it just to give my mind some kind of rationalization for wanting you."

She nearly laughed. "And you need a rationalization…why?" She didn't wait for him to answer. She spilled what had been gnawing away at her for hours. "Because of something I said about Greg while I was under hypnosis?"

Jason loosened his grip a little so he could inch back and meet her gaze. "You don't remember?"

"No, and believe me, that's not a good feeling because I'm afraid I said something that hurt you."

"You said you didn't love Greg."

"I didn't love him," she added cautiously.

He paused. And paused. It went on so long that Lilly started to squirm, both literally and figuratively. "When you told Greg that, you said the two of you argued and that he accused you of not loving him because you were attracted to…well, me."

Oh. She'd really turned chatty during that hypnosis. Chatty about things she'd barely admitted to herself.

"Is it true?" Jason asked.

Well, at least she didn't have to think about the answer. "It's true."

And she braced herself for the fallout. What he must think of her. Sleep with one brother while being attracted to the other. Not exactly the start to a long-term relationship—if that's what either of them wanted, that is.

Was it?

Lilly didn't get an answer to her question. Nor did she get any fallout from her chatty revelation during hypnosis. There was a knock at the door; Detective Albright waited for Jason to tell her to come in before she opened it. Jason and Lilly had plenty of time to move away from each other. However, she figured they both looked guilty of something. She certainly felt guilty, anyway.

"Sorry to disturb you," Detective Albright said. "But I just got a call from the security guard at the gate. Your former nanny, Erica, just tried to use her access code to get inside the gate."

"The security company changed the codes," Jason advised.

Albright nodded. "Don't worry. Erica didn't get in, but she says it's urgent and that she's not leaving until she speaks to you."

But the detective wasn't looking in Jason's direction when she said that. She aimed the *you* right at Lilly.

Chapter Thirteen

"You don't have to do this," Jason reminded Lilly. He didn't know why he was wasting his breath—it was obvious he wasn't going to get her to change her mind—but he wasn't backing out of the garage to leave for her physical therapy appointment until he'd gotten his point across.

And his point was that meeting with Erica just wasn't a bright idea.

"We have to drive through the security gate anyway," Lilly explained. "Erica will be there, and she wants to speak to me. We might as well take a minute or two to see if she'll confess to trying to kill us. Then, you can arrest her."

Somehow she managed to keep a straight face when she said that, but Jason doubted he could do the same. "And you see what's wrong with that logic, right?"

"You mean, the possibility that this is a ploy so she'll have another opportunity to try to kill us?"

"Yes, that."

Lilly shook her head. "You think Erica's willing to do that in broad daylight in front of witnesses and with you carrying that big gun in your shoulder holster? Because she must have known you'd be with me."

He didn't want to point out that if Erica was enraged, on a rampage for revenge, then she might not be thinking straight. Still, it didn't make sense for Erica to start shooting at them. Even though she was a suspect, Jason had her at the bottom of the list. The woman had loved and cared for Megan for more than eleven months. She'd been a good nanny. It was hard to dismiss that. He only hoped his dismissal wasn't a mistake that he'd come to regret.

Realizing he'd just talked himself into this meeting with Erica, he cursed under his breath, backed out of the garage and started the drive to the security gate.

"What if this isn't about a confession?" he asked, playing devil's advocate both with Lilly and himself.

"What else could she possibly have to say

to me? Don't answer that," Lilly quickly insisted. Probably because she knew this might not be some earth-shattering revelation or confession but a rehashing of the uncomfortable goodbye they'd already had with Erica.

Jason hoped that was all there was to it.

When he approached the gate, Jason looked around for Erica's car but didn't see it. In fact, he saw no vehicles other than the white truck with the security company's logo. Instead, Erica was standing on the concrete platform in front of the small structure that housed the guard.

Jason stopped next to her, but he didn't get out. He lowered the window and then slipped his hand inside his jacket in case he'd been wrong about her and had to reach for his gun.

"Erica," he greeted. He made a visual check and didn't see any weapons. Thankfully, she wasn't dressed for concealment. Hard to conceal anything while wearing shorts and a cotton top that barely made it to her waist. Still, that didn't mean she hadn't stashed a weapon in her vehicle. "I don't see your car. How did you get here?"

That question seemed to unnerve her. She shifted her feet and folded her arms over her chest. "I parked up the street. I figured I'd use my access code to walk in because if you saw my car pulling up in front of your house, you probably wouldn't have even answered the door."

He would have, but he darn sure wouldn't have let her inside. "What's this visit all about?" Jason asked.

Erica barely spared him a glance, her attention focused on Lilly. "I don't know if you're still trying to take Megan away from Jason, but I've been doing some thinking. And I've decided that I can't give her up."

Jason hadn't forgotten about the custody issue, but he no longer believed that Lilly was out to gain total custody of Megan. Or maybe that was wishful thinking, too.

"Was that just an FYI comment?" Lilly asked. "Or did you have something specific in mind?"

"Oh, it's definitely specific. I found a lawyer who's willing to help me petition a judge for visitation rights. I raised her. I was more than a nanny." Now her gaze drifted in Jason's direction. But it not only drifted; it lingered a bit and turned into a heart-tugging stare. Jason didn't want Erica's pain and emotion to get to him, but he wasn't impervious to it, either.

"A lawyer?" Lilly repeated in a flat tone.

"I won't be shut out of Megan's life, understand? And I won't stand by while you continue to endanger her."

That was not the right thing to say. Jason tried to hold on to his temper. "Care to explain that?"

Erica pointed to Lilly. "Someone's trying to kill her, and that person isn't likely to stop until he or she succeeds. That means, every minute she spends in your house is a minute where Megan is in danger. Believe me, my lawyer plans to let the judge know that." Erica didn't wait for them to respond. Nor did she issue a goodbye. She spun around and hurried away.

"Well, that was pleasant," Lilly said sarcastically. "You were right. No confession."

While he wasn't happy about that, Jason was pleased that it hadn't turned into a shoot-fest. Still, Erica's threatened lawsuit and criticism of Lilly was yet something else on a plate that was already way too full.

"No judge will give her visitation rights," Jason assured Lilly. But he wasn't so sure. As a cop, he'd seen judges do the surprising and the unthinkable. And this certainly qualified as unthinkable.

"Erica's right, you know," Lilly concluded as Jason drove out the gate and onto the street.

He checked the rearview mirror but didn't see Erica anywhere. "About what?"

"About me endangering Megan."

Jason knew where this was going and tried to stop her, but Lilly was obviously determined to be heard.

"It's not only irresponsible of me to stay at your house," Lilly conceded, "it's selfish. And it's wrong."

Oh, how a few days could change things. A week ago he would have jumped at the chance to have Lilly far away from Megan. Now he wasn't jumping. Well, not that kind of jumping, anyway. "Please don't tell me you're even thinking about leaving."

"I shouldn't be just thinking about it. I should be doing it."

"No, you shouldn't."

"You think I want to do this?" she asked.

"It'd break my heart to leave, but if this is the way to keep Megan safe, then I'll start packing as soon as we get back."

Jason glanced at her. "And you're letting Erica's opinion convince you to do this?"

She turned in the seat to face him. "Erica only stated the obvious."

Okay. He had some talking to do here. He only hoped he was persuasive enough. "Think this through, Lilly. If you leave, what's to keep this monster from trying to use Megan to get to you?" Jason didn't stop there. "And what if your ploy works? What if by leaving, the killer comes after you and succeeds? What then? Greg's already dead, so you've essentially made Megan an orphan."

"She has you," Lilly pointed out after she swallowed hard.

"She has you, too, and it'll stay that way. There's no safe place. Not for Megan. Not for us. The only thing we can do is work together to catch this guy. That's it."

Lilly shook her head, turned back around in her seat so they no longer had eye contact. "I want to agree with you, because I want to be with my daughter, but I think we have to consider my leaving as the right thing to do."

Jason didn't miss that *be with my daughter* part. He couldn't blame Lilly for not including him. Heck, he couldn't even include himself.

Not for a real, permanent commitment anyway.

But maybe something else.

Less than a half hour earlier, Lilly had admitted that she was attracted to him. He was attracted to her. They even cared for each other. To what extent that caring was, he didn't know. However, he did know that they both loved Megan.

Maybe that was enough.

Maybe with Erica's legal threat, it had to be enough. This was definitely a united-we-stand kind of situation.

"We could get married. For Megan," he suggested. Jason didn't even look at Lilly. He kept his attention fastened to the road. However, he had no doubt he'd just shocked her to silence.

Unfortunately he didn't know how to continue after that. Since they'd kissed and come close to having sex, such a proposal might seem an insult. Of course, offering her a real relationship would be a lie. He cared for her. But they weren't in love with each other.

Still…

He glanced at her to see if she was dumb-struck at his pseudo-proposal, but instead she had her attention fastened to the side mirror. There wasn't alarm in her eyes, but just the fact that she was staring at it had Jason whipping his gaze at the rearview mirror.

There was a car behind them.

Not a maroon four-door. Thank God. It was dark green, and it had heavily tinted windows so he couldn't see the driver inside. It was the only other vehicle on the road. And it was following a little too closely for his comfort.

Hell.

Was this yet another threat? Was this the person who was after Lilly? And had he already let him or her get the advantage by getting so close?

Testing a theory he didn't want to prove correct, Jason sped up a little. So did the other car. And then he knew for a fact that this was not going to be fun.

"Is your seat belt on?" he asked Lilly.

"Yes." He didn't have to see her face to know what she was feeling. He heard the fear and the concern in her voice. He tossed her his phone. "Call for backup and get down on the seat."

The words had hardly left his mouth when the car behind them sped up. But it didn't just involve speed. It was a lurching motion, and the vehicle rammed into them, jolting their SUV forward so that Jason had to fight to maintain control.

His adrenaline level was already high, but that sent it soaring. He went into combat mode and hoped his training and blind luck would be enough to get them through this.

There was another ram. Harder than the first. Then another. Jason cursed. His SUV jerked to the right when he strayed onto the rim of the sidewalk. He corrected and then corrected again so that he wouldn't broadside a car parked on the otherwise empty residential street.

He forced himself to stay focused. Forced himself to rely on his training. Especially since it might be minutes or even longer before backup arrived. He scanned the area to make sure there were no more immediate threats or innocent bystanders who could be hurt. It was as clear as it possibly could be: no bystanders, which also meant no witnesses. Whoever was in that car behind them probably knew that.

"Should I try to drive so you can shoot at him?" Lilly asked.

He didn't have to think about that. "Too risky." Jason wasn't just referring to discharging his firearm in a residential area, either. He was referring to Lilly. Her body probably wasn't strong enough to make the switch to the driver's seat, much less keep control of the SUV.

And speaking of keeping control, Jason latched on to the steering wheel to brace himself for the next slam. It wasn't a moment too soon. The car behind them crashed into the back bumper, and Jason let the forward momentum career him into a side street. Fighting with the steering wheel, he spun his vehicle around, screeched to a stop and drew his weapon.

"Get down on the floor!" he shouted to Lilly.

Thankfully, she listened, though by getting onto the floor, it didn't mean she was safe. Not even close. Bullets could easily penetrate the metal and glass, and she could be hurt.

Or worse.

Jason was counting heavily on that worse not happening.

Using the meager cover of the steering wheel and the dash, he ducked down just slightly in the seat and slid his finger over the trigger. He was ready to fire.

Ready to kill, if necessary.

But he didn't get a chance to make that kind of life-and-death decision. The other vehicle didn't wait. The driver slammed on the accelerator and sped away.

Jason threw off his seat belt and jumped from his SUV. He aimed his weapon and got off one shot. The bullet hit the back tire, but the driver kept on going.

He re-aimed and was ready to deliver a second shot when he saw a female jogger move onto the sidewalk right next to the escaping car.

Cursing, Jason lowered his weapon. He wasn't finished. He was going after the SOB responsible, and one way or another, this would end *now*.

Chapter Fourteen

Lilly had no doubt about what she would see when she walked into Jason's office.

Yep. No surprises.

His jacket was slung over the back of his chair. His black T-shirt was now tucked. His hair mussed, no doubt from where he kept plowing his hand through it in frustration. And he was still on the phone, barking out orders to one of his fellow officers and sprinkling those orders with demands and profanity.

With the phone squashed between his shoulder and his ear, he was pacing. Like a riled tiger ready to strike. He was also checking the magazine of ammunition in his backup gun. His primary weapon, his Glock, had been sent to headquarters, because he'd discharged it in the line of duty. There'd be reports to do. Questions and more questions. An investigation. All necessary because of that one futile shot Jason had fired into the tire of their attacker's vehicle.

She stood there, using the door frame as support, and waited for him to finish his latest call. Every muscle in his body was iron-stiff, and she could practically see flames in his eyes. Lilly understood the pacing and even the ammunition check. However, while she was feeling the same emotions as Jason, he obviously had her beat in the intensity department.

Lilly could thank a hefty amount of fatigue and Megan for the semicalmness she was now experiencing. She'd just fed her daughter a bottle and settled Megan into the play-room/panic room. That brief time with her child had lowered Lilly's anxiety level enough for her to try to help Jason lower some of his.

A huge undertaking, no doubt.

He'd already done her a favor just by staying put. She knew how hard it'd been for him to do that. His every instinct had probably demanded that he go in pursuit of the car that'd rammed them.

But he hadn't.

After a fierce battle with himself, and with

her not-so-gentle coaxing, Jason had taken them back to his house so he could make an initial report of the incident. And so he could sequester himself in his office to make phone calls. Unfortunately, both the initial report and the phone calls had only made the tension in him worse.

"Is something wrong?" Jason asked the moment he ended his call.

"Everything's fine. Megan's playing with Detective O'Reilly," Lilly told him. "She's discovered the joys of pulling off her socks and tossing them into the air." She hoped the news about Megan's cutesy milestone would cause him to relax a bit.

It didn't.

"And the other officer arrived to relieve Detective Albright?" Jason asked, reholstering his gun.

"Yes, about ten minutes ago." Despite the feeling that she was now living in a police compound, she welcomed the officer's presence. Having three cops in the house might allow her to breathe a little easier. Or at least it would take some of the pressure off Jason so that he might not feel totally responsible for Megan's and her safety. Of course, he'd no doubt feel that way if they had the entire police force in his living room.

"I don't want Megan out of the playroom," Jason continued. "And I also don't want either of you in any part of the house without an officer nearby, got that?"

"Agreed." He'd already told her that twice. With Jason's anxiety obviously near the boiling point, Lilly figured she'd hear it again soon.

"By the way, how are you holding up?" Jason asked. Not just a question, though. It was edgy and raw, like everything else about him.

Lilly sighed. Much more of this and he'd explode. It was time for action. Or rather, a good old-fashioned lecture. She shut the office door and leaned her back against it. "I want you to stop beating yourself up about all of this."

"I can't," he snapped. "This is my fault."

That answer didn't surprise her. "Noo-oo, it's not. It's the fault of that idiot in the other car."

Jason grumbled something she didn't want to interpret and started to pace again. "We can't keep going through this. We've been lucky, but we might not be so lucky next time. That's why I'm arranging for a safe house. An undisclosed location that only a handful of trusted cops will know about. It should be ready tonight. It'll have a solid security system. Plus, another officer and I will be with Megan and you at all times."

"That's good." Well, the security part was, but it meant they'd have no privacy. No real life. No real anything. They'd be on hold and all because of some unknown moron who wanted her dead. That moron wouldn't be shut away in some safe house, either. He or she would be out there, free, doing everything possible to find them.

So, just how safe would a safe house be?

"Nothing about this is *good*." Jason shoved his backup weapon into his ankle holster. "It's too little too late. Just how many sleepless nights will you have because I haven't been able to catch this guy?"

That did it. Lilly had had enough. She couldn't bear to see him like this. "How many sleepless nights will *you* have because of this nightmare that I brought to your doorstep?"

He dragged his hands through his hair again. "I'm not in the mood for sympathy and comfort."

"Tough. You're going to get it anyway." She snagged him by the arm when he started to pace by her.

Jason stared at the grip she had on him and then lifted his eyes to meet hers. "My advice? Back off, Lilly. I've got a lot of dangerous energy inside me right now, and you don't want any part of this."

"Oh, really? That sounds like a challenge," she said, because she thought they both needed a little levity.

The levity backfired.

Big time.

Adrenaline was high. Emotions, higher. Coupled with the attraction between them, touching him was indeed a dangerous prospect. She immediately thought of ways to defuse that tension. Well, one way in particular. Too bad it would have huge consequences.

Lilly tried to fight her way through her exposed emotions, the leftover fear and the fatigue. She tried to do the logical thing.

And failed.

When she realized her body wasn't going to cooperate with her attempts to think this through, she finally said to heck with it. She looked at Jason. At his face. At those intense gray eyes that were piercing into hers. And she knew exactly where this moment had to go.

Suddenly everything was crystal-clear. Razor-sharp. Powerful and honed. Like the energy spearing through her. She had the power to help him, to help them both. Human contact, human touch could undo a multitude of troubles. She wouldn't even think about the new troubles that it would create.

Before she could change her mind, or before he could stop her, she tightened her grip on his arm and pulled Jason closer.

Closer.

Closer.

Until his chest brushed against her breasts.

He stared at her, the intensity in his eyes going up another serious notch. "Think this through," Jason managed to say. Not easily, though.

"I already have."

Without further words, she put her mouth to his.

And Lilly kissed him.

OH, MAN. This was *so* not good.

At least that's what Jason's mind told him.

But the rest of him heartily disagreed. It wasn't just *good*. It was better than good. Exactly what he wanted.

Just when he thought he couldn't take any more without breaking, Lilly stopped the kiss. Maybe to catch her breath. Maybe to give him time to do something about this. And she stood there, staring at him, looking better than any woman had a right to look.

Her hair was loose, resting at her shoulders on the thin straps of her mist-green dress. And her eyes were making offers that he couldn't refuse. Everything about her, that face, those eyes, her mouth, called to him.

Cursing himself, cursing their situation, cursing fate and just plain cursing, Jason did the very thing that he knew he'd almost certainly regret. He gave in to the moment. Gave in to all the wants and all the primitive needs that were clawing their way free. He gave in to *her.*

He pulled Lilly to him. Knowing there was no turning back. Not caring. And knowing he would care and have regrets later. Still, that didn't stop him.

With the slight shift of movement, their bodies came together again. His pressed against hers. Her right leg wedged between his. They adjusted. Moved. So they could get as close as two people could possibly get. So they could do something about this ache. This need.

And the battle started.

Her mouth took his. Her lips moving against his. Not a soft gentle kiss of comfort. Not this. There was no comfort in the sensual moves of her mouth. This was all heat, fueled with lethal adrenaline and emotion.

Because he wanted more, and he wanted it now, he somehow managed to get her dress unzipped. It wasn't easy. His hands weren't too steady, and Lilly made things more difficult with the kisses that she was lavishing on his neck. A definite sensitive spot for him, and she'd figured that out right away. She kissed, using her tongue, pulling him tightly against her body. Drowning him in her scent.

Jason shoved her dress down to expose her bra. White lace. Definitely not modest, either. It kicked up his heart rate. Revved his body. Nearly made him beg. He took a moment to admire it and the woman beneath it before he caught the straps and lowered them, as well, to expose her breasts. She was small, firm.

Perfect.

Keeping his gaze connected with hers, he slowly lowered his mouth to one of her rosy nipples and nipped it with his teeth. A sharp gasp and Lilly grabbed him by the hair and pulled him to her, forcing him, until he took that nipple into his mouth. Leaving it shiny wet and pebbly hard, he gave the other one the same attention. She gasped. A sound of pleasure. And actually did some begging of her own.

It still wasn't enough.

Jason had to have more of her. All of her. Lilly obviously felt the same because she suspended her kisses, and struggling for position, went after his T-shirt. Like his, her movements were fast and frantic. It was a race. Against what, Jason didn't know, but it didn't matter. All he knew was that they had to have each other.

While she dragged his T-shirt off him, Lilly moved against him. Body against body. It was like striking a match. What little control he had left went straight out the window. He grabbed her by the hips and brought her roughly and precisely against him, aligning them.

"Jason," she whispered. She made a throaty sound of approval. "Yes."

He'd never been happier to hear a yes, and he was especially pleased that it had an urgency to it. He completely understood that urgency.

"I can't wait," she said. And she meant it.

Lilly kicked off her strappy sandals and went after his zipper. She succeeded. And she didn't stop there. Locking her arm around his neck, she freed him from his boxers and took him into her hand. Jason was fairly sure his eyes crossed, and the pounding pulse in his ears made it seem as if they were surrounded by primitive war drums.

"Now," she insisted.

Jason obliged. He hoisted her up and wrapped her long, lean legs around his waist. He pulled off her lace panties and in the same motion, repositioned her so that her back was against the door.

Though his vision was blurred, he forced himself to focus so he could watch her. So he could see her face. Her eyelids lifted when he pushed into that heat. Into her. Into her moist, welcoming body. And a kiss caught their collective sighs of pleasure and relief.

The kiss lingered a moment so she had time to adjust to him. But Lilly obviously felt she needed no such adjustment or time.

"Don't stop," she insisted. Lilly shoved herself against him. Sliding against his erection. Taking every inch of him.

Jason took everything she was giving, as well. The passion. The sensations of their bodies joined.

No longer wary of her response, he pinned her hands to the door and was pleased when she jerked and twisted against him. Her legs tightened around him. Forcing him closer. Forcing him to penetrate her even deeper.

They matched each other. Move for move. Trying to hang on to every second, every sensation. Until the friction and the pleasure were unbearable. Until all Jason could see, hear, feel, smell and taste was Lilly. She became the pinpoint of his focus, of his universe.

She became everything.

She whispered his name in rhythm to the frantic strokes. Jason waited a moment. Holding off as long as he could so he could hear every syllable, so he could watch his name shape her lips.

"Now, Jason," she said.

He agreed. It was time. His body couldn't hold back any longer. Not with this intensity. Not with the fierce need he had for her. So, with Lilly's whispered pleas brushing against his mouth, with her heartbeat pounding against his, with their bodies damp with sweat sliding against each other, Jason gave them both what they needed.

THE SENSATIONS slammed through her, leaving Lilly hazy and feeling as if everything were right with the world. She didn't leave that hazy place immediately. She stayed there a few moments, letting her body slowly come back to earth.

Even though earth wasn't where she wanted to be.

She wanted to linger in that haze. And to linger in Jason's arms, a safe place where there were no problems and no one was trying to kill them.

"That was amazing," she whispered.

Even though Jason was looking directly into her eyes, he blinked as if trying to focus. And probably was. She wasn't anywhere near 20/20 yet, either. Sex with Jason

apparently had the potency to blur vision—
in a good way, of course.

His breath was coming out in hot gusts. "I
can't believe we just did that."

"Please don't tell me you have regrets."

He shook his head and eased her legs from
his waist. "No condom."

Those two words rang through her head
and she nearly fell when she put her feet back
on the floor. "Oh, sheez."

"But you're right, it was amazing. And
this might be the lust talking, but it was
worth the risk."

Lilly thought so, as well. She only hoped
they both felt that way days or even weeks
from now. She had too much on her mind to
consider an unplanned pregnancy.

"I don't even know if it's the wrong time
of the month," she concluded. "But with everything my body's been through, I doubt
I'm ovulating."

Famous last words?

She hoped not. And while she was hoping,
she added other issues to that proverbial list.

"I've considered just beating around the
bush with this, but since time seems to be an
issue here, I'll just come out and ask." Lilly

fixed her dress, sliding it back into place, and she discretely stepped back into her panties. She didn't continue until she was done and until Jason's gaze met hers. "Having sex with me wasn't your way of working out our custody issues, was it?"

Jason blinked again, but this time he actually focused. "I'm going to pretend you didn't ask that."

"All right, so if that wasn't about custody, was it anger sex?"

He zipped his jeans as if he'd declared war on them. "Are you trying to pick a fight?"

"No. But it probably seems that way to you. I'm actually trying to understand what just happened."

"You tell me, Lilly. If I'm not mistaken, you're the one who started it by kissing me." He held up his hand in a defensive, wait-a-minute gesture. "Oh, are you trying to tell me it was sex to stop me from leaving?"

She was on shaky turf. "It started that way, yes," Lilly admitted. "But then it sort of took on a life of its own, wouldn't you agree?"

Jason was no doubt spoiling for a fight. Not necessarily with her. But with the person who'd been trying to kill them. Still, he couldn't help those emotions erupting. And she was right in his path.

"I'm not sorry for what happened," she said. However, it didn't ring true. Not totally. She might not be sorry, but she'd no doubt regret it. Sex complicated things, but it wasn't that complication that bothered her the most.

It was her feelings for Jason.

Mercy. How was she supposed to deal with all the other things they were facing when all she wanted was to pull him back into her arms and kiss him again?

Lilly gave that question some thought, and she didn't like where that thought was leading. This sexual encounter hadn't solved anything. In fact, it'd done the opposite. It'd made her realize just how empty her life would be without him.

Yes, empty.

Jason made her happy, and as silly and cliché as it sounded, he completed her. She understood that now. Understood what was truly at stake here. Not just Megan. Not just Jason. Her future with both of them was at stake.

Before Lilly could even begin to think

about spilling what was in her heart, there was a tap at the door. "Jason?" It was Detective O'Reilly. "Did Lilly tell you that the other officer is here to assist with security?"

"She told me." Jason lifted an eyebrow. Lilly lifted hers, as well. "What about the suspects? Have they been located?"

"Not yet."

That sent Jason to the door. He opened it with a fierce jerk. "*None* of them?"

Lilly had to hand it to Detective O'Reilly. He looked as if he wanted to take a huge step back, but he held his ground. "Wayne Sandling and Raymond Klein aren't at their residences. Erica Fontaine isn't at her hotel. And there's still no luck finding Ms. Davies, dead or alive."

Jason obviously didn't care for that information. "What's the latest from the lieutenant?"

"I just got off the phone with him," O'Reilly said. "He needs you to come down to headquarters and fill out your report about discharging your weapon."

Lilly groaned and shook her head. "Can't that wait?"

"I don't want it to wait." Jason reached

for his jacket. "Now that the other officer is here, I'll do the report and then see if I can find our suspects."

Lilly went to Jason, blocking his path toward the door. "I thought I'd talked you out of doing this."

In fact, that was what she'd done for the first half hour after they'd arrived back at the house. However, Lilly wasn't under any misconception that she'd been able to convince him to stay put. His staying probably had less to do with her convincing than it did with the fact that his departure would have left Megan and her alone at the house with just one cop—O'Reilly. Now that the other officer was in place, that was no longer an issue.

"I'm going to find them," Jason insisted.

Her hands went to her hips. "Excuse me, but how do you plan to do that?"

"I'd like to know that, too," Detective O'Reilly added. But his comment only earned him one of Jason's prizewinning glares.

"I don't know how just yet, but I can't sit here and do nothing." Jason made a vague motion toward the outside. "I want to find them, and I want them to tell me everything they know about any of this."

A dozens arguments came to Lilly's mind. Good arguments, too. But she didn't get to voice any of them. Jason pressed a kiss to her mouth and moved her aside. O'Reilly didn't hold his ground this time. He stepped out of the doorway so Jason could leave.

"I have to do this," Jason said as his goodbye.

And because Lilly knew she couldn't stop him, she just stood there and watched him walk away.

"Oh, God," she whispered as a prayer.

The fear and dread were immediate. A sickening feeling that knotted her stomach. The taste was suddenly bitter in her mouth. Because Lilly had a feeling that something terrible was about to happen.

That was her first thought.

Quickly followed by another that was equally unnerving.

She hoped she got the chance to tell Jason something that she'd just realized.

She was in love with him.

Chapter Fifteen

"Have I mentioned that this is probably a huge waste of my time and yours?" Jason heard Sgt. Garrett O'Malley say.

The question didn't stop Jason. He simply gave his phone headset an adjustment so he could respond, and he kept on driving through the upscale neighborhood that Wayne Sandling called home. "Yeah. But a possible waste of time is better than nothing."

O'Malley made a sound to indicate he wasn't so sure of that.

Jason countered it with a grumbling sound of his own. "I guess that means there's no sign of Raymond Klein?" Jason asked.

"Nothing. And I do mean nothing. Not even a dog walker or a jogger." Garrett was several miles away, driving through Klein's neck of the woods, and though they'd both been at it for nearly an hour, things weren't looking good.

Their suspects had seemingly disappeared.

Of course, in Corinne Davies' case, she was possibly dead, but that left three others—Wayne Sandling, Raymond Klein and Erica Fontaine. Jason wanted to speak to all of them, and he didn't want to wait another minute to do it. Too bad waiting seemed to be on the agenda tonight.

"Why don't you go home to Lilly and Megan?" O'Malley suggested. "I'll keep looking around. If any or all of our suspects surface, I'll call you."

Considering that it was the sergeant's night off and that he was doing this surveillance as a favor, Jason didn't want to take him up on the offer. Still, he didn't want to leave Megan and Lilly alone any longer. Not that they were alone, exactly. There were two officers standing guard at the house. Jason knew the cops would do their job, but it wasn't personal for them.

It *was* personal for him.

He would do whatever it took to protect Megan and Lilly.

"Thanks," Jason told O'Malley. "I think I will go back to the house and check on things. I won't be long. Oh, and call me the minute you have any information."

"Will do. And while you're checking on things at home, why don't you get some rest?"

Before he ended the call, Jason assured him that he would. It was a lie. There'd be no rest tonight. Not with the suspects at large. Not with so many things unresolved.

Yes, this was indeed personal.

On the drive home, that one sentence kept going through his head, and though he knew he should be focusing solely on catching a would-be killer, he couldn't help but think of what had happened earlier.

He'd had sex with Lilly.

Unprotected sex at that.

If there was a name worse than idiot, that's what he should call himself. No, he didn't regret the sex part. Though he should have regrets. He didn't.

He couldn't.

Making love to her, even in that heated, frantic rush was exactly what he'd dreamed about doing since Lilly had first set foot inside his house. And that need he had for her didn't have anything to do with Megan. What had happened between Lilly and him was about two people who couldn't keep their hands off each other.

Part of that disgusted him. The lack of control. Yet, another part of him wanted to lose control with her all over again.

Hopefully, this time with a condom.

It had been reckless to have unprotected sex. Here she was, just recovering from the coma. She would need lots more physical therapy before she was a hundred percent, and yet he'd risked getting her pregnant.

He frowned at the reaction that caused deep inside him.

A baby. A brother or sister for Megan. Why did that sound so damn appealing when it could cause nothing but problems for Lilly? She was just getting used to being Megan's mom. She didn't need any more pressure.

She didn't need him.

There.

That was it.

The niggling thought that kept at him. Day by day, Lilly was getting back to her old self, and once she was no longer in danger, she would be on the road to a full recovery. She'd resume her business, balance it with motherhood. Lilly was a pro at balancing. At efficiency. At being self-reliant.

She wouldn't need him.

But he would still need her.

Worse, that need was growing, and he was certain it wouldn't simply go away. With that thoroughly depressing revelation, he took the turn into his neighborhood and stopped at the security gate.

"Please tell me it's been a quiet night," Jason said to the guard as he punched in his security code.

The guard nodded. "Just a few people coming home from work and a pizza delivery."

That snagged his attention. "You checked them all out before you let them in?"

"I did. I had the residents show picture IDs, and I called the folks that ordered the pizza and had them confirm it."

Though Jason was appreciative of those security measures, he didn't relax. He drove home, wondering how in the name of heaven he was going to put an end to all of this.

Because without an end, Lilly and he didn't stand a chance at having a beginning.

He approached the house with his cop's gaze on full alert. And maybe it was that full alert that had him concerned when he noticed that the lights were off. Then, he checked his watch.

10:00 p.m.

Well past Megan's bedtime, and as tiring as the day had been, it was no doubt past Lilly's, as well. He pulled into the garage and sat there for a moment, listening. He was still listening when the sound shot through his SUV.

The sound nearly caused him to jump out of his skin. Before he realized it was his phone ringing.

"Sheez. Settle down," he warned himself. He'd snap if he kept up this intensity.

"It's Garrett," Sgt. O'Malley said when Jason answered the call. "And before you ask, no, I didn't find any of the suspects. But we've had a Corinne Davies sighting."

Well, Jason hadn't counted on hearing that, ever. "I take it she's alive?" He used the remote to close the garage door and got out of his SUV.

"According to her neighbor, yeah. He says this afternoon he saw Corinne going into her house through the back door. We sent a unit out to see if she was there, but there was no sign of her."

Which made her all the more dangerous. Well, dangerous if she was guilty of anything. Maybe Corinne was simply a victim, like Lilly. A case of learning a little too much and now having to pay the consequences.

"Thanks for the update," Jason said, clicking the end button on his phone. He unlocked the door that led from the garage into the house and went inside.

And he came to a complete stop.

Two things immediately struck him as totally wrong. The security alarm didn't kick in, and the house was much too quiet. It was bedtime, he reminded himself. But that reminder did nothing to stop the slam of adrenaline. That instant jolt of fear.

His stomach dropped to his knees.

Jason pocketed his cell and drew his weapon. Because the sense of urgency was growing stronger with each passing second, he hurried. Running, he made his way through the utility room and into the kitchen.

No one was there. Including the officers he'd left to guard the place. But there was a half-eaten sandwich and a nearly full glass of milk sitting on the counter.

He considered calling out to them, but his instincts told him it was already too late for that.

Trying not to make a sound, he made his way across the kitchen and to the hall that led to the back of the house. With each step, his heart pounded, his focus pinpointed and his body prepared itself for the fight. Maybe, just maybe, he wasn't too late.

But he was.

Jason confirmed that when he saw Lilly.

There she was. At the end of the hall. Just outside the door of the playroom.

The only illumination came from the night-light on the wall halfway between Jason and her. But it was more than enough for him to see the stark expression on her face.

The fear.

No. The terror.

That's when Jason realized she wasn't alone. There was someone behind her. With a gun that'd been rigged with a silencer.

And the gun was pointed right at Lilly's head.

LILLY THOUGHT she couldn't have possibly been more frightened, but she wrong. Her fear went up a significant notch when she saw Jason step into the hall.

Another minute or two, and this could possibly have been avoided.

Of course, another minute or two, and she might have been dead, but at least Jason wouldn't be in danger.

He was definitely in danger now.

Jason stood there. Not frozen. Not panicking. He inched toward them, his gun aimed and his wrist bracketed with his left hand. He was ready for anything.

Well, maybe not this.

There was no way he could be ready for this.

"Put down the gun," Jason said, his voice hardly more than a whisper. Probably so that he wouldn't wake up Megan. Lilly was praying the same thing. She wanted to keep her daughter sheltered from this.

"I can't," the woman behind Lilly answered.

Now, that stopped Jason. Lilly completely understood his reaction. She'd experienced a similar reaction about ten minutes earlier when she first realized that someone had gotten into the house.

And *who* that someone was.

"Erica?" Jason questioned.

Behind her, Lilly heard Erica's breath shudder. Not good. While Jason seemed relatively unruffled, she couldn't say the same for Erica. It wasn't just the woman's voice that was shaking. Erica was shaking, too. Lilly didn't care much for a jittery person with an equally jittery hand holding a gun to her head.

"She's trying to kidnap me," Lilly confirmed, not surprised that her own voice was trembling. Oh, she was scared. But she was even more frightened of staying put, where Erica could do heaven knew what to Jason or Megan.

There were worse things than dying.

Lilly knew that now. And losing Jason and Megan would be far worse than anything Erica could do to her.

"Is Megan okay?" Jason asked. No calmness that time. He had to get his teeth unclenched so he could speak.

"She's asleep," Erica volunteered. "I wouldn't hurt her."

Not intentionally, anyway. But Lilly knew

if bullets started flying, then good intentions weren't worth anything.

"Put down the gun, Erica," Jason warned, the grip tightening on his own gun.

"I can't. Not now. I have to stop this. I have to stop her."

"None of this is Lilly's fault. All she did was wake up from a coma."

"All she did was ruin my life," Erica snapped. "I love you, Jason—"

"Put down the weapon," Jason repeated. "And think this through. Megan is in that room right next to where you're standing with a loaded gun. If she wakes up, she'll be scared. Is that what you want?"

"No." Erica repeated it several times, her voice becoming edgier with each syllable. "All I want is to leave. With Lilly. I have to take her with me."

"You don't have to do anything but put down the weapon and step to the side." Jason inched closer.

"Stop," Erica said, pushing the gun even harder against Lilly's temple.

Jason stopped, and Lilly could almost see him thinking this through. She only hoped he had a better solution than anything she'd been able to come up with—which was exactly nothing. If she fought back, Erica might shoot and accidentally hit Megan. If she remained passive and cooperated, the same might happen.

"How did you get in here, anyway?" Jason asked Erica.

Lilly shook her head, indicating that she didn't know. She'd literally come out of the playroom to discover that she was looking down the barrel of a gun.

"I paid off the pizza delivery guy. He let me hide in the trunk of his car. Then I used my key to get in the house," Erica explained. "I turned off the security system."

Even in the darkness, she saw the flash of anger in Jason's eyes. "Where were the two police officers during all of this?" he snarled.

"I, uh, used a stun gun on both and tied them up."

There, she saw it. The skepticism on Jason's face. It would have been next to impossible to get close enough to two trained officers and surprise them with a stun gun. Lilly didn't know for sure, but she suspected both officers were probably dead. And that meant Erica had shot them with her gun fitted with a silencer.

Would she try to do the same to Jason?

It was too painful for Lilly to consider. Here, she'd just gotten back her life, and she might lose everything.

She frowned.

Listening to herself.

What the heck was she doing standing here, waiting for the worst to happen? So what if Erica had a gun on her? She had something that Erica didn't. She loved Jason and Megan. And it wasn't Erica's kind of psycho possessive love, either. It was the kind of love that could make her do anything to protect them.

Anything.

Lilly stared at Jason. Hoping that her now unyielding expression conveyed that she was about to do something to get them out of this dangerous situation. He obviously got the point, and didn't approve, because he narrowed his eyes.

Jason's change in facial expression must have alerted Erica because Lilly felt the woman go stiff. "Don't do anything stupid," Erica warned.

Lilly didn't have anything stupid in mind. She hoped.

Of course, anything could qualify as stupid if it wasn't successful.

Lilly gave Jason one last glance, and she gathered all her fear, all her energy, all her anger, and focused those emotions right into the elbow that she rammed hard into Erica's stomach.

Erica gasped and made a kind of garbling sound that indicated she was fighting for air. Good! Lilly did some fighting of her own. She turned, ignoring the wobble in her legs, and slammed her hand against the gun to try to dislodge it. Erica somehow kept control of it.

Jason charged toward them and, fearing that Erica would turn her gun on him, Lilly grabbed the woman's wrist and put it in the tightest lock she could manage.

Erica reacted. Mercy, did she ever. With the strength of ten men, she shoved her entire weight against Lilly, off-balancing her. Not that it was that hard to do. Wobbly legs didn't give her much of an advantage.

Lilly felt herself falling, and she couldn't do anything to stop it. She reached out for anything, but her hands only grabbed at the air. She landed hard on the floor just inside her bedroom.

Thankfully, Jason didn't fall right along with her. He launched himself at Erica. They both crashed into the wall. But the crash didn't cause Jason to loose focus. When the scuffle was over, Lilly could see that he now controlled both weapons.

The breath of relief that Lilly was about to take stalled in her lungs. Before she could take that breath, she heard the sound behind her.

But it was too late for her to react.

Too late to stop what was happening.

The arm curved around her neck, and Lilly felt the barrel of a gun jam into the back of her head.

Chapter Sixteen

Jason had known this situation could quickly get out of hand. That was why he'd been so anxious to get the gun away from Erica. During all his concern about doing that, while also being worried about how to keep Lilly and Megan safe, he'd overlooked one important detail.

That Erica might not be working alone.

And she wasn't.

He became painfully aware of that when he came up off the floor with Erica in tow, and he saw Lilly. She didn't have a triumphant, we-got-her expression. But a frightened one.

Lilly was in the doorway of her bedroom, and even though the room itself was pitch-black, Jason could see the shadowy figure behind her. It took a moment to figure out why he couldn't distinguish any facial features.

The person was wearing a ski mask.

In addition to the ski mask, he or she had a gun aimed at Lilly. Like Erica's weapon, it, too, was rigged with a silencer. So, who was the brains behind this operation: Erica, or this person who had seemingly come out of nowhere?

The person didn't speak, but Jason saw the arm-grip tighten around Lilly's neck, and he saw the slight gesture with the gun. The gesture was directed at Erica.

"Jason, give me those," Erica insisted, obviously responding to the gesture.

She reached for the guns that Jason had in his hands, but he sidestepped her. He could have easily brought her down with one hard punch. Or with one shot. And, man, he wanted to do that after what she'd just pulled. However, the person holding Lilly would retaliate.

"Think of Megan," Lilly whispered to him. A warning for him to do whatever it took to prevent gunfire. Drywall wasn't much protection against bullets, and he couldn't risk Megan getting hurt.

But he could say the same for Lilly.

He couldn't risk her life, either.

Now, the problem was how was he going to convince her to play it safe? That elbow ploy had worked on Erica, but Jason had a feeling that the success had been more luck than anything else. He didn't want to rely on luck to keep his family safe. And it didn't matter that Megan wasn't his biological daughter, or that Lilly wasn't his wife, they were his family in every way that counted.

"I want the guns," Erica prompted, motioning for Jason to hand them over.

Jason said a prayer and made his move. He reacted as fast as his hands could react. He tossed one of the guns aside and, in the same motion, he latched on to Erica. He shoved her in front of him and put the remaining gun to her head.

"Drop your weapon," Jason ordered the person in the ski mask.

The person made a slight huffing sound. "Not on your life. Or rather, should I say, not on Lilly's life."

Jason didn't have any trouble recognizing that voice, and obviously neither did Lilly. Her eyes widened a fraction, and her mouth tightened. "Raymond Klein," she mumbled.

Another huff and Klein loosed his grip around Lilly's neck so he could peel off the ski mask. Jason almost made a lunge for him then and there, while he was briefly distracted with the mask removal, but never once did Klein take the gun from Lilly's head. Jason figured he was fast, but he wasn't faster than a finger already poised on the trigger.

"I'd hoped to avoid all of this," Klein said in a discussing-the-weather tone. He aimed his attention at Erica. "We need to do this quickly. We don't want those two cops waking up."

"They're alive?" Jason asked.

"For now. I used a stun gun on them once Erica had them amply distracted. Then, I gave them each a dose of barbiturates that should keep them out for a while longer."

Jason processed that information. And it didn't process well. With that ski mask, the two cops probably hadn't seen their attacker's face. But they'd sure as heck seen Erica's.

Jason figured that meant Klein planned to set Erica up so she would take the blame.

Erica obviously hadn't figured that part out yet.

"Drop your weapon, Detective Lawrence," Klein insisted. "Or I'll kill Lilly before you've even had a chance to say goodbye to her."

Jason wasn't immune to that threat. It cut through him like a switchblade. But he pushed aside his fear and concern and focused on being a cop. Somehow he had to get Lilly and Megan safely out of this.

"Have you forgotten that I could do the same to Erica?" Jason fired back at Klein.

"Be my guest," Klein calmly said.

Because he still had hold of Erica, Jason felt her body tense. The quick, almost frantic intake of breath was an obvious clue that she'd just realized she was expendable.

"What are you saying?" Erica asked, frantically shaking her head. "The plan was to kidnap Lilly. That's it."

"The plan has changed," Klein informed her. "I can't leave witnesses behind, now, can I?"

"No!" Erica shouted. "We were going to

kidnap Lilly, that's all. You said you could get her out of the country and put her somewhere so she wouldn't be able to come back. And she'd be out of the way so I could move back in here with Megan and Jason."

"I lied," Klein said, and he angled his eyes toward Jason. "Put the gun down now."

Jason knew he couldn't do that. "No way. You've already said you won't leave any witnesses."

"Go ahead, Jason," Lilly said. "Shoot him."

"If he does, you'll die," Klein reminded her.

"And then Jason will kill you," Lilly countered.

Jason must have conveyed his displeasure about that because Lilly nodded, as if trying to convince him that she was doing the right thing. "This way, one of us will survive," she told him. "Do it for Megan."

It was dirty pool. And it was a useless plea. Because if Lilly had her way, that plea would get her killed.

He had no plans to let her die.

Jason quickly went through the possible

scenarios; he didn't like any of them. The risks were sky-high, but they were risks he couldn't do anything about. Doing nothing was just as risky. So he said another prayer and hoped like the devil that he could pull this off.

He shoved Erica forward, slamming her into Lilly. It had the domino effect that Jason hoped it would. Both Lilly and Erica flew back into Klein. All three went backward onto the floor.

Jason didn't waste even a second. With his gun aimed and ready to go, he launched himself at Klein so he could kick the gun from the man's hand.

He failed.

Jason heard the sound. Not a blast. But a muffled slash of noise. It didn't have to be loud, though, for it to be deadly. Because Jason knew that Klein had just fired the gun rigged with the silencer.

LILLY KNEW that sound.

A gunshot.

It instantly fed the terror that was already snowballing inside her. That bullet could have hit Jason. Or Megan. God. She couldn't lose them.

She came up off the floor. Or rather, she tried to, but a punch to her jaw sent her sprawling. Lilly felt the warm, wet sensation on the side of her face but ignored it so she could launch herself at Klein. She couldn't let him fire again. No matter what the cost, even if it meant dying, she wasn't going to let him shoot Jason or Megan.

In the darkness, she saw the tangle of their bodies. Hers, Jason's, Klein's and Erica's. Erica and she were on the floor, and Klein and Jason were standing, more or less, and were about to square off in what looked to be a gun battle.

Except Jason was no longer armed.

Somewhere in the scuffle, he'd lost his gun. Oh, God. That meant Klein would no doubt try to kill Jason.

Lilly ignored the stinging pain in her jaw and reached out. She managed to grab Klein's leg, and she tried to drag him to the floor with her. She wasn't successful, but for a split second, she'd distracted him.

Klein looked down.

Aimed his pistol right at her.

And he would have shot her point-blank if Jason hadn't rammed his body into the man. Somehow, Jason stayed on his feet, and it became a struggle for control of the gun.

Lilly decided to put the odds in their favor. She spotted Erica's weapon on the floor and scrambled toward it. Her legs suddenly felt like a deadweight, and she cursed her lack of mobility. It was no longer just an inconvenience. It was a handicap that could get them killed.

If she let it happen.

She wouldn't.

She fixed the image of Megan and Jason in her mind, and she used that image, her love for them, to force herself to move forward. One inch at a time.

Behind her, she could hear the sounds of a struggle. Fist against muscle. Did that mean that Jason had somehow managed to get the gun away from Klein? Or, heaven forbid, had Erica joined the fight?

With her heart pounding and her breath so thin that her lungs felt starved for air, Lilly stretched out her hand and scooped up the gun from the floor. She came up and was face-to-face with Erica.

"I can't give up Megan," Erica said as if it would change what Lilly was feeling.

It was on the tip of Lilly's tongue to tell her that she had already lost Megan, but the slash of movement from the corner of her eye had her looking up. At Klein.

Once again, he had the gun pointed at her.

"If you move, Detective Lawrence, I'll kill her."

Normally those words would have terrified her beyond belief, but this time they didn't have the effect that Klein had probably intended.

Why?

Because Lilly heard Megan. Her baby was not only awake, she had begun to cry, and those cries were quickly turning to sobs.

Lilly made eye contact with Jason. Mere seconds. To let him know this was about to end. He gave a crisp nod.

Her cue.

Or at least Lilly made it her cue. She ignored her limp muscles and pulled back her leg. She focused all her energy and rammed her foot into Klein's thigh.

Klein reacted all right. He howled in pain. But that didn't stop him from re-aiming his gun. Jason yelled for her to move, but she couldn't, and everything seemed to crawl in slow motion. She heard the sound, like someone blowing out a candle, and felt the sensation of pressure against the right side of her head. It didn't stay merely a sensation.

It quickly turned to pain.

And Lilly realized she'd been shot.

She dropped back onto the floor. Around her, there was a flurry of motion. Jason cursed and grabbed Klein, knocking the man's gun away. Jason seemed enraged, and he landed a hard fist in Klein's face.

Klein went down like a rock.

Jason didn't stop there. He snatched up his Glock and aimed it right at him.

"Move and I'll kill you." That was all Jason said. All he had to say. Because anyone who heard the threat knew that he meant it.

Lilly wanted to help Jason. She wanted to make sure that neither Erica nor Klein had managed to regain control of one of the weapons. She also wanted to thank Jason for saving her life.

But she couldn't do any of those things.

The dizziness came with a vengeance. The room began to spin out of control, and though she was aware that Jason was speaking, she couldn't understand what he was saying. Worse, she knew she was losing consciousness. Lilly fought it.

But she lost.

Because she had no choice, she shut her eyes and the darkness came again.

Chapter Seventeen

Jason had already said at least a thousands prayers for Lilly, but he added another one before he opened the door to her hospital room. He braced himself for the worst, and he hoped for the best.

He got the best.

There she was, not in bed, but sitting on the edge of it, dangling her bare feet off the side. She had a small white bandage on her forehead. That was it. No bruises. No other indication that Klein's bullet had come much too close to killing her.

Things had not seemed so promising during the frantic ambulance ride from his house to the hospital. Then, Lilly hadn't been conscious, and she was losing blood from the head wound. In those moments, Jason would have bargained with anything or anybody just to have her safe.

"You're here." She smiled at him.

That smile warmed the bitter cold that had seeped into his body. "I'm here."

Because he didn't trust his legs to move, he stood there a moment and savored the view. "The doctor said the bullet didn't do any serious damage, just a graze, and that you were going to be okay."

Lilly gave him a contemplative look. "You didn't believe him?"

"I had to see for myself."

Her smile returned. "You can see for yourself if you come closer."

Jason did. No uncertain legs this time. Now that he knew Lilly was truly all right, he made it to her in just a few steps. He leaned down, put his arms around her and pulled her to him.

"I'm fine, really," she promised.

He eased back so he could kiss her. Jason meant for it to be quick and reassuring, but Lilly obviously had other plans. She slid her arms around his neck and kissed him back. She lingered a bit and left them both a little breathless. That was fine. Jason preferred her kisses to breathing any day.

Lilly ran her tongue over her bottom lip and made an *Mmm* sound to indicate she liked the taste of him there. "How's Megan?"

He had to get the goofy smile off his face before he could answer. "She's out in the hall with Detective O'Reilly. I wanted a few minutes alone with you, first."

"Uh-oh." There was suddenly strain in her voice, on her face. "Bad news?"

Some of it, yes. But other parts were very good. "Klein is behind bars," Jason said.

Lilly pumped her fist in the air. "Hallelujah. Did he happen to say why he wanted to kill me?"

Her question had come easily, but Jason didn't have such an easy time with the answer. Every memory of what Klein had said and done would haunt him. "He did. He's talking because he's trying to make a deal to cut down his prison time."

Lilly's relief faded. "He won't be getting out soon, will he?"

"Not for at least thirty years." Forty, if the D.A. had his way. "Thanks to a tough interrogation, Klein admitted to trying to kill you and running Greg off the road that night."

"I see." She cleared her throat and blew

out a choppy breath. "So, he killed Greg?" she clarified, wanting to be sure.

Jason nodded.

The relief returned to her face, but it was intensified. She even blinked back tears. Jason understood her reaction. For nearly two years she'd blamed herself for Greg's death. For two years he'd blamed her, as well. That blame belonged solely on Raymond Klein's shoulders.

"They can get Klein for manslaughter for Greg's death," Jason explained. "But they'll charge him with attempted murder and kidnapping for what he did to you." He paused. Heck, he wasn't sure he could say this out loud, but he knew that Lilly would want to know. "Klein wanted you dead because he thought you would eventually remember that he was the one who ran you off the road that night."

She flexed her eyebrows. Paused. "Well, at least it's over." Lilly stared at him. "It is over, isn't it?"

He nodded. "Erica will be arrested as soon as she's out of the hospital."

"She was hurt?" Lilly immediately asked.

"Not badly. Klein shot her in the arm. Like

you, she'll make a full recovery, only she'll be doing time while she's at it. For attempted kidnapping, among other things. The D.A. isn't pleased that Erica endangered the lives of a child and several police officers."

Jason wasn't pleased about that, either. In fact, it might take a couple of lifetimes for him to get over the sheer terror he'd felt when he'd realized that Megan could be hurt and that Lilly had been shot.

"More good news," Jason continued so he could lighten the quickly darkening mood. "Corinne surfaced. She got scared and went into hiding when someone tried to kill her."

"Let me guess—Klein was behind that, as well?"

"He was. He wanted to make sure she didn't go to the police with the info she found in some old files. Klein wasn't just altering bids, he was creating false contracts for repairs and maintenance to municipal and state buildings. He was getting paid a small fortune, too. And he's the one who stole her car so he could try that break-in at the security gate. His attempt to kill Corinne will tack on another few years to Klein's prison sentence."

Jason considered that the end of his official update, and he took her by the hand.

"Oh, no. Not more bad news." Lilly groaned.

"I hope not. I'm hoping you'll consider it good news." He rethought that. "Or I at least hope you'll consider it."

Because he was so close, he could see the pulse jump on her throat. "Okay, you have my attention."

"Don't say no until you've heard me out." Jason gathered his breath and his courage. This was really going to hurt if she said no. "When Klein had his gun on you—"

"This doesn't sound like the start of good news," Lilly interrupted.

"It is. Trust me. When I realized your life was in danger…" He had to take another moment. More breath gathering. Another prayer. "I also realized that I wanted you to marry me."

She blinked.

Not exactly the reaction he was hoping for.

"Did you hear me?" he asked. "I want us to get married."

Still no answer. She waited for what

seemed to be an eternity before she finally spoke. "For convenience? Because of Megan?"

He made a deep sound of frustration. "No way. In fact, I can promise you that being married to me will be anything but convenient. I can also promise you that I'll do anything to make you happy."

Another blink. No smile. Just a blank stare. "Anything?"

"Anything. And I mean that. Groveling, foot massages, great sex—"

"How about love?"

Oh.

Jason tried to sort through what he'd already told her, but there was a big jumble in his head. He blamed it on the nerves and the total lack of sleep. "Didn't I mention that I'm in love with you?"

She shook her head. "No."

Oops. That was a biggie. "Well, I am."

No blink this time. But her breath trembled and her eyes watered.

"Oh, man." Jason pulled her into his arms. "You're crying."

"They're happy tears, I promise."

Happy tears, he mentally repeated, and it

took several tries for it to sink in. The relief he felt was overwhelming, and he hoped he didn't disgrace himself by crying, too. Since he didn't want to risk that and since she still hadn't said yes, he kissed her. Really kissed her. He took all his feelings, all his love, and poured it all into an intimate show of affection.

"Yes," she whispered against his mouth.

"Yes?" And he hoped he hadn't misunderstood her.

"Yes, because I'm in love with you, too."

Okay. He mentally repeated that to himself, as well.

Jason's first reaction was to whoop for joy, grab her and swing her around in circles. Since she might not be ready for that, he laughed. Hugged her. And kissed her. This was what he wanted, and until a few short hours ago, he hadn't even known it.

"I do have some…news," Lilly said, inching just slightly away from him.

Because of all they'd been through, his first thought was that this wasn't going to be good. Lilly's puzzling expression only added to his reaction. "You're not changing your mind about marriage?"

"No. It's not that. It's this whole pregnancy thing."

"Excuse me?" he asked, certain he'd missed something. "You're pregnant?"

She shook her head. "No. I talked to the doctor about our unprotected sexual encounter, and he did a few tests. Turns out that I wasn't in the whole ovulation zone." She paused. Stared. Moistened her lips. "This is going to sound a little crazy, but I was actually a little disappointed."

So was he. A real shocker of a reaction. "We can try again when the time is right. Hey, I'm always up for a round of unprotected sex."

She smiled. "Against the door of your office."

"Anywhere. Anytime," he promised, smiling with her. His mouth came to hers again. A kiss. And that kiss might have lasted for hours if there hadn't been a knock at the door. "Are you ready for a visitor?" he heard Detective O'Reilly say.

Jason looked back at his fellow officer and spotted not just O'Reilly but Megan, who was already making her way toward them.

Since Megan was a little wobbly, Jason

went ahead and picked her up and brought her to the bed. O'Reilly, probably sensing the need for privacy, stepped back into the hall and shut the door.

Lilly wiped away her happy tears and reached out for Megan. "You know what, your da-da and I are getting married. That's a great deal for all of us."

Jason didn't let go of Megan just yet. He whispered in her ear what they'd been practicing on the drive over. Megan looked up at him and beamed with one of those precious smiles.

"Ma-ma," she babbled.

Since the first attempt was aimed at him, he turned Megan in Lilly's direction. "Ma-ma," Megan repeated. Not just once. But she strung those syllables together, giggled at her accomplishment and made a dive for Lilly. She landed in her mother's arms.

More happy tears came, and Jason had to choke back a few of them himself.

"Da-da," Megan said, snuggling against him.

"Jason," Lilly whispered, snuggling, too. And Jason knew that this was the life he'd always wanted. He reached for both of the ladies that he loved, gathered them into his arms and held on.

* * * * *

Don't miss Delores Fossen's next romantic suspense, THE CRADLE FILES, coming in July 2006 only from Harlequin Intrigue!

HARLEQUIN®
INTRIGUE®

WE'LL LEAVE YOU BREATHLESS!

If you've been looking for thrilling tales of
contemporary passion and sensuous love stories
with taut, edge-of-the-seat suspense—then
you'll love Harlequin Intrigue!

Every month, you'll meet six new heroes
who are guaranteed to make your spine tingle
and your pulse pound. With them you'll enter
into the exciting world of Harlequin Intrigue—
where your life is on the line
and so is your heart!

THAT'S INTRIGUE—
ROMANTIC SUSPENSE
AT ITS BEST!

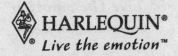

HARLEQUIN®
Live the emotion™

www.eHarlequin.com   INTDIR104

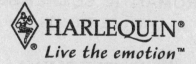

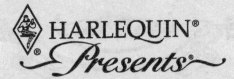

HARLEQUIN®
Presents®

The world's bestselling romance series...
The series that brings you your favorite authors,
month after month:

Helen Bianchin...Emma Darcy
Lynne Graham...Penny Jordan
Miranda Lee...Sandra Marton
Anne Mather...Carole Mortimer
Susan Napier...Michelle Reid

and many more uniquely talented authors!

Wealthy, powerful, gorgeous men...
Women who have feelings just like your own...
The stories you love, set in exotic, glamorous locations...

HARLEQUIN®
Presents®

Seduction and Passion Guaranteed!

Harlequin Historicals®
Historical Romantic Adventure!

*From rugged lawmen and
valiant knights to defiant heiresses
and spirited frontierswomen,
Harlequin Historicals will
capture your imagination with
their dramatic scope, passion
and adventure.*

*Harlequin Historicals . . .
they're too good to miss!*

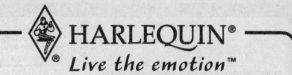